BEYOND REMORSE/COBRA

Serpents MC Las Vegas

BARBARA NOLAN

Gabby,
Happy Reading!
B. Nolan

D1264472

Published by: Barbara Nolan

Edited by: Lisa Cullinan

Proofread by: Rose Holub

Cover Model: Shane MacKinnon

Photographer: Furious Fotog

Cover Design/Formatting,: Mayhem Creations

CJG Consulting

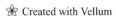 Created with Vellum

Dear Readers:

I am so blessed to be able to do something I love, while also giving enjoyment to others. Once again I want to thank the many people in the Indy community for their generosity and shared knowledge. The main players are mentioned in the credits of this production, but I'd also like to thank my beta readers. Their suggestions and contributions are invaluable. Beyond Remorse is especially close to my heart as the main character suffers with something I have battled in life. Many of us are struggling with different obstacles, and I feel it is important to address them in a way that shows strength, determination and compassion.

I hope you enjoy Cobra and Sheena as much as I enjoyed writing them.

Love,

Barbara

CHAPTER ONE

R emorse. Everyone felt bad about some shit thing they did or didn't do. Guilt that niggled their nerves during the day and plagued their sleep at night. Cobra knew all about the nagging, gnawing weight that never relented, and only grew heavier day after fucking day.

Cobra experienced a love/hate relationship when visiting Danny. He loved seeing his brother's smile knowing how much these visits meant, but he hated the anguish that tore at his gut. The deep-down torment that Danny was held prisoner in his own body ripped Cobra apart daily.

Every time he looked into Danny's bright, blue eyes a turmoil of emotions twisted him up. If only he'd gotten to the trailer sooner. If only he'd taken Danny with him that night. If only his father wasn't an abusive shit. The 'if only's' tried to destroy him, but he fought against their damning recriminations.

Redemption.

Cobra sucked in the dry desert air. A strange mix of dust and whatever tropical flowers were planted along the pathway that led from Brookdale Rehabilitation Center. His booted feet couldn't move fast enough. You'd think after all these years the pain and regret would've faded, but no, it only increased. A burden that pummeled him daily and easily crushed his six foot three, two hundred and twenty pounds of fuck you attitude.

Finally, reaching the parking lot, he threw his leg over the Harley and looked away from the two-story, white building on the outskirts of Las Vegas. His phone vibrated in his jeans pocket and he scanned the ID, then swiped at the screen. "Yeah."

"Hey, fucker," Python yelled over the background noise. "Get your ass to the Gold Mine. You're missing all the fun."

"On my way." Cobra disconnected the call, shoved the phone into his pocket, and kicked the bike to life. He revved the engine loud and long, knowing his brother could hear it and picturing the smile on his face.

He backed his bike out of the space, hit the throttle, and sped out of the parking lot aware that he would be right back here tomorrow and all the days that followed.

Sacrifice.

The usual ache in his chest reminded him that he would never be a good man. Sure, his biker brothers respected him, and swore their allegiance to the club, but that didn't change the way Cobra felt about himself. He could play all the mind games he wanted, but the fact remained, Danny was strapped into a wheelchair because of him.

SHEENA SURVEYED the crowd at the Gold Mine. She didn't know much about biker life, and although she'd spent the last five years in Las Vegas, she'd never ventured into the bar owned by the Serpents MC right off the Strip.

She wedged herself through the crowd of well-wishers until she was next to her best friend, Daisy. "Can't believe you're really married."

Daisy flipped up her hand where an exquisite diamond ring and wedding band flashed under the lights. Joker, her new husband, leaned in circling his arms around Daisy's waist. "I can't believe this beautiful woman agreed to marry a thug like me."

Joker's voice was laced with love, humor and shots of tequila. Since they'd entered the bar the drinks had flowed freely, and everyone was buzzed. Joker's words reminded Sheena of all the couple had been through over the last few months. After outsmarting a drug lord in Miami, and almost losing his son in the crossfire, Joker and Daisy deserved some peace and happiness.

Daisy kissed her new husband full on the lips, then wriggled out of his hold, and leaned into Sheena to be heard over the ear-splitting music. "Have you had a chance to check out some of these guys here. Super hot."

"You're a married woman." Sheena shot back, knowing full well that Daisy was playing matchmaker.

"It's time for you to move on." Daisy and Sheena's gaze drifted across the crowded bar to Seth, standing apart from the crowd, brooding.

"I know," Sheena agreed. "I've given him chance after chance and he never takes the bait."

"His loss."

Sheena silently agreed. Back in the day, her, Seth, and Daisy ran some of the biggest cons in Vegas. When their boss got arrested for tax evasion, Daisy fled to Miami for a while.

Seth and Sheena got out of the game, donned pirate costumes and waited tables at the Pirate's Cove, a theme bar on the strip. Complete with a pirate ship decor, pirate music and a gang plank that she would've gladly jumped off. Mind numbing, low paying work, and a boss who didn't question the severe gaps in her work history. Gaps that she had no intention of explaining to anyone, ever.

The only illegal act she indulged in now was charging the ridiculous prices for the fruity drinks. A big step down from the luxurious life of a high-end con woman.

She'd grown to love the desert city that saved her and allowed her to bury her East Coast identity while carving out a brand new life for herself.

TWENTY MINUTES LATER, Cobra pulled up outside the Gold Mine determined to put his depression on hold and celebrate Joker and Daisy's wedding.

He entered the bar with the usual fist bumps from the regulars and the rest of his biker buddies. A welcome fit for the president of the Serpents MC Las Vegas chapter, although most times he felt like a fraud, not the outlaw biker with the fuck you attitude they all expected.

Cobra joined Joker and Daisy at the long table they'd set up for the newlywed couple. He flicked his wrist and two waitresses appeared at his side. "Another round. He motioned around the table. "Fuck, bring two more rounds. We got a lot to celebrate."

Whoops and cheers rang out until Cobra waved his hand around. "Shut the fuck up." When the cheering subsided Cobra turned to Joker and Daisy as the waitresses placed shot glasses in front of them. Cobra stood and raised his glass. "Here's to the married couple. I don't know how an ugly mutherfucker like you landed such a babe, but congratu-fuckin-lations."

4

The brothers pounded on the table until Joker grabbed Daisy around the waist and hauled her onto his lap. They gazed into each other's eyes and even Cobra could see the connection. Joker kissed her deep and long while his hands roamed over Daisy's body.

Joker and Daisy did the deed Vegas style. She'd surprised him by setting up the ceremony at a drive-up chapel with a Harley-Davidson officiate. A fitting venue for an outlaw biker, even though Joker'd sworn off the outlaw part. He'd come out to Vegas with Daisy after his New York club fell apart. Cobra liked Joker's kick ass attitude and commitment to family, even offered him a patch with the Serpents, but Joker claimed he wanted out of the life. Cobra wasn't buying it.

Either way Joker had clearly met his match with Daisy. She went toe to toe with him, and the way she came through for him here in Vegas definitely proved she had his back.

What would it be like to feel that way about a woman or to have a woman feel that way about him? Better question, what the hell was wrong with him and all this damn deep thinking lately? Fuckin' ridiculous.

In true biker fashion the party geared up fast and after a few shots Sheena, Daisy's friend and some of the other women took over the dance floor with moves that made his dick want to jump out of his jeans. But it wasn't the sinful moves Sheena was popping, it was the almost innocent expression on her face, like she didn't realize she was so fuckin' sexy. Or that she was giving every guy in the room blue balls, including him.

Running Ecstasy, a high-end strip club owned by the Serpents, Cobra was usually immune to woman's bodies and the way they moved, and it had been a long damn time since watching a woman dance gave him this kind of a reaction.

What really bugged him though was the magnetic way his eyes followed her every move. He'd never had a reaction to a woman like this before and he couldn't decide if it was because she was hotter than hell, or because either intentionally or unintentionally she ignored him.

Cobra hated waiting—Waiting in traffic, waiting for a phone call, waiting in a line, but waiting for a woman to notice him—Nah, that was bullshit. Women came onto him and definitely didn't ignore him, but there were some things you just couldn't control, some things that got under your skin. The old wanting what you couldn't have, and since Cobra was used to having it all, this scenario messed with his brain.

Some whoops and fist pumps drew Cobra's attention to the back of the bar where one of the girls had stripped off her top while climbing on top of a table. Yeah, not a party until somebody got naked.

He shifted his gaze to Joker and Daisy making out in the corner. Cobra smirked as he made his way toward them. He plopped down next to Joker and shoulder butted him. Yeah, he was being a prick.

Joker untangled himself from Daisy and narrowed his eyes. "You enjoy being a dick?"

Cobra flashed his shittiest smile. "Yeah, kinda do." His gaze wandered to Sheena on the dance floor. A few of the other girls followed the topless chick's lead, but not Sheena. All her clothes on and she still remained the sexiest woman on the dance floor.

Joker leaned in. "Instead of eye fuckin' her like a puppy dog why don't you talk to her."

Cobra dragged his eyes away from Sheena's bangin' body and glared at Joker. "The fuck?"

The annoying cocksucker was right. He'd had eyes on

Sheena from the first time he'd seen her with Joker and Daisy a week before the wedding. The way her wild tangle of jet black curls fell around her face. He asked Joker some indirect questions, but he'd been evasive. Just as well, she wasn't part of the biker life and with all the shit he had going on, he didn't need any more complications.

Celebrating Joker and Daisy's wedding had thrown him and Sheena together again, but waiting for a woman to take notice that he'd been tracking her all night pissed him the fuck off.

"You've been scoping her out all night." Joker raised his chin. "Why don't you stop acting like a pussy, and go for it"

This was his place, his territory and if he wanted something he'd take it. One way or the other. The waitress brought over more shots. Cobra downed his, slammed the glass onto the table, and pushed away from his chair. He stormed across the dance floor snatching Sheena by the arm, then leading her to the bar.

When they got to the bar, Sheena yanked her arm out of his grasp. "There are subtler ways of getting someone's attention."

"I'm not into subtle." Cobra flagged down Rattler tending bar, then turned to Sheena. "What do you want?"

"I've moved on to water."

Cobra screwed up his face. "Bring two shots of tequila and leave the bottle."

"Right, boss." Rattler spun away from them and a few seconds later there were two tequila filled shot glasses and an uncapped bottle.

"Do you enjoy being a dick?"

Cobra did a double take. "Shit, you're the second person that's said that to me tonight?"

"You know what they say. When more than one person tells you something it must be true."

Oh shit, he loved a woman with fire. Before the night was over he would have her under him, screaming his name, and begging him to never stop.

"C'mon, let's celebrate Joker and Daisy's true love." The sarcastic lilt he added to his voice got her attention.

"And I suppose you don't believe in anything as sappy as love."

He smiled at her sass and tried to think of another way to piss her off because the way her eyes lit up when she was dishing it out sent a jolt right through his gut.

"The only thing I believe in is the here and the now." He challenged her, pinning her dark eyes that were almost black until she looked away and focused on the bar top.

"We need limes and salt." Sheena motioned to the tequila. "If we're going to do this, we should do it right."

Cobra's mind immediately locked on those pouty lips of hers sucking on a lime or sucking on his—

"Don't you agree?" Her teasing voice jarred him out of his sextasy. He would've loved to palm his dick and move it away from the irritating zipper of his jeans, but there was no way he could make that move discreetly.

Cobra slapped his palm against the bar. "Hey, Rattler, salt and limes." Two seconds later they magically appeared.

Cobra zeroed in on her pink tongue as she licked the back of her hand then sprinkled salt on it. She grabbed up a lime wedge and paused. "What's with the snake names, Cobra, Rattler?"

"We are the Las Vegas Serpents." The last thing he wanted to talk about was the history of the club or the fucked-up way it got its name.

"So, everybody has a snake name?"

Cobra pointed to her shot. "Why don't we save the history lesson for later."

She eyed the shot glass, then downed it in one.

She motioned to his. "I'm not doing this alone."

Cobra slammed the shot, circled his hand around her wrist, sucked the salt off her hand and lingered. "Hmmm." He snatched up a lime and sucked out the juice. "Best fuckin' shot I've had in a long time."

"That's because you did it right."

"Nah, doin' it right would be you laid out on this bar and me sucking that tequila off that sweet skin of yours."

She rolled her eyes. "Are you always such a charmer?"

He rubbed at the stubble on his chin and let her have the last word. "Joker says you live in Vegas."

"Been asking around about me, huh?" She waggled her eyebrows.

"I like to know the people who are in my bar."

"Your bar?"

"Owned by the Serpents MC and since I'm the president . . ." His fingers were aching to reach out and touch the wild tangle of curls that brushed against the swell of her breasts. "How come I've never seen your sweetness in here before?"

"Not usually a fan of bikers or their bars." She pointed to the back of the room. "But since Daisy married one."

"What's the matter? We too wild for you?"

"No, more like too prehistoric. I'm not into men who think they can own their women."

"Whoa." Cobra threw up his hands. "Let's back this up. I ain't looking to own anything but my bike."

"Fine."

"Yeah, fine." Cobra poured two more shots and held hers up to her. "Why don't you tell me what's with the guy at the other end of the bar who keeps giving us the fisheye?" Cobra jerked his chin in Seth's direction.

"I've got absolutely no idea." Sheena ran her fingers threw her hair.

Cobra had no intentions of getting into any drama tonight, but he'd play along for now. He slung his arm around her shoulders and leaned in. "So, maybe it's time I show you that not all bikers are the same."

She laughed at his innuendo and her lush hair brushed against his stubble.

She raised the shot glass and a male hand circled her wrist. "Don't you think you've had enough?"

The guy finally decided to grow a pair.

"What're you, her fuckin' babysitter?" Cobra sneered.

Sheena drew in a deep breath. "Relax Seth, I'm fine."

"Yeah, relax Seth." Cobra pulled Sheena in closer. "In other words get the fuck outta my face."

CHAPTER TWO

Seth mashed his lips together and Daisy actually felt sorry for him. Seth's tall, rangy body was no match for Cobra's thick, corded bulk or his heavily muscled arm that he'd draped over her shoulders. The last thing Sheena wanted was Seth and Cobra getting into a pissing match, but she'd given Seth so many chances to make his move and now when someone else showed interest he decided to step up. Too damn late. Sorry, not sorry.

Seth angled his body toward Sheena. "I'm not leaving you here with him."

Cobra kept a firm hold on Sheena. "You do realize you're standing in a Serpent's bar, right?"

"You can do better than him, Sheena."

"Take a look around, asshole." Cobra dropped his arm from Sheena's shoulder and stepped to Seth. "All I have to do is flick my wrist and you'll have five guys bigger than me whooping your ass."

Seth stepped off but kept his eyes on Sheena. "I'll go but I think you're making a big mistake."

Cobra flicked his wrist and as he predicted a huge guy appeared at his side. "Yeah, Prez?"

Cobra jerked his chin at Seth. "Get this asshole outta here."

Sheena gripped Cobra's arm. "Don't hurt him."

"All right, Python, you heard the lady, hands off." Then he turned to Seth. "I ever see your ass in here again and I won't be so nice."

Python pushed Seth toward the door and Cobra leaned against the bar.

Sheena brushed her hand against his forearm. "Seth is harmless."

"Nobody's harmless, babe. So don't get it twisted."

Probably good advice, although coming from an outlaw biker that seemed like an oxymoron.

"I just meant that he's not a fighter."

"Right, well then he oughta learn to keep his mouth shut or he's gonna end up missing some teeth."

She stroked Cobra's forearm until he faced her. "Thank you for not hurting him."

He focused on her hand. "He's gone, babe, we don't have to keep this goin'."

"What?"

"Making your boyfriend jealous."

"He's not my boyfriend."

He nailed her with a curious expression. "I saw the way you were looking at him and how you checked out his reaction every time I touched you."

She'd underestimated this rough biker with the movie star face. Much more observant than she gave him credit for. "He's not interested."

"Didn't look not interested to me." Cobra crossed his arms

over his massive chest challenging her. Her eyes drifted to the letters scrolled onto the underside of his forearms, but she couldn't make out the words. She tilted her head and then realized he mimicked her. "I think if we kept that going awhile longer he might've actually found his balls and dragged you outta here."

She focused on his words and reality hit.

"So all this was just—"

Cobra's lips quirked. "You tell me, babe. I was just giving you what I thought you wanted."

She cocked her head trying to figure out his game. He sure seemed interested to her, so was he really that cagey or was he just flipping the script to save face.

"Sensing other people's vibes keeps me alive, and what I saw here was a guy who needed a little push." Cobra flashed a sneaky grin. "And there ain't nobody better at pushing than me."

"Thank you, I think." Now she was confused, so she went with casual and flip. "I guess he's just not that into me, as they say."

"Nah, could be a lot of things. Probably intimidated by the way you look."

"The way I look?"

"All tough bitch, bangin' body with an ass that's made to be gripped with both hands, and hair that should be fisted and pulled."

Sheena's throat closed up at the visual and her eyes flicked to the tequila.

Cobra pointed to the bottle. "You look like you could use another?"

"No." She pushed the glass away to make her point. Creepy how he'd seen that, knowing exactly how his mini fantasy affected her.

Cobra's phone lit up on the bar. He swiped at it and his neck stiffened. "Yeah." Cobra barked into the phone.

"He say what he wanted?" Cobra asked, then waited.

"I'm on my way." He pocketed his phone and turned to her. "Gotta go."

"Sure." Disappointment surged through and her insides cringed at the unexpected reaction.

"Hope it works out with you and . . ."

"Seth," she offered.

"Yeah, right."

She wanted to say more. Like, I wasn't just using you to make Seth jealous, and most frightening of all, I don't want you to leave yet. She gripped the bar to keep her traitorous hands from reaching out and brushing her fingers against the warm, muscled skin of his forearm. Or flip his forearms over so she could read the words etched across his smooth skin. She clenched her jaw so she didn't yell out over the music. "Please stay."

He stared at her while she engaged in her mental volley-ball like he sensed her conflict. Very unsettling

"Since bikers or their bars ain't your thing there's prob-ably no chance of seeing you again—So, have a good life."

"Thanks." She flashed him her mind-fucking smile. The one that always worked, except now, with this sex on a stick biker. His face remained expressionless for another second and then he winked at her. As if to say, yeah, I'm reading your mind and there isn't a damn thing you can do about it.

Cobra swaggered out of the bar without looking back, and Sheena stared after him. Inches had separated them before, and still she couldn't figure out his game. She was the master of the scam and yet he'd played her, which left her wondering what exactly made him tick. And who was on the other end of the phone that made him leave without a moment's hesitation.

PATRICE, the manager of Ecstasy, the Serpents strip club in North Las Vegas, only called when there was a problem, so to hear from her at 11:30 on a Saturday night was not good.

Cobra revved his Harley and weighed Patrice's words until the neon lights from the Strip faded behind him. Vinnie Black, the sketchy Las Vegas fixer, was waiting to see him. Vinnie had a rep for getting things done. Illegal things. Hard to believe the man could make a living in a state that legalized gambling, prostitution and weed, but Vinnie was notorious for being knee deep into all kinds of shit. Mostly keeping other people's secrets.

Vinnie's more lucrative dealings were running some of the biggest underground poker games on the Strip. Games he organized for high rollers who'd been banned from the legit clubs for numerous reasons. Then Vinnie took his cut off the top, and always made a profit. Not such a surprise when he had the best card mechanics in the state dealing from the bottom and everywhere in between.

Cobra pulled his Harley into his spot at the back of Ecstasy and prepared himself. He'd never trusted the designer suit wearing douche, and now old grudges and recent problems made them more enemies than business associates, but Cobra would play it cool and feel out the sneaky bastard.

Cobra tipped his chin to the two bouncers at the door and entered the dimly lit club. Steven Tyler blared out of the state-of-the-art sound system as Crystal, one of the headliners, made love to the pole. Cobra ran Ecstasy like any other business, paying taxes, complying with the ABC laws and making sure he never gave the great state of Nevada a reason to close him down.

The girls were all Victoria Secret look-alikes with strict

rules about conduct. Customer relations took on a whole new meaning when you were taking your clothes off for money, but every girl knew that the club had their back. Cobra didn't allow anyone to touch the girls on stage, and every private room had a bouncer and plenty of cameras to make sure all the men got was a lap dance. In return he demanded that his girls stay clean. No drugs, no booze and no sex in the club. Absolutely no sleazy shit allowed.

"Hey, baby." Patrice handed him a glass of Jack Daniels. "I hope I didn't tear you away from anything important." Her gaze lingered, searching.

To anyone else that would've seemed like an innocent statement, but Patrice was a lot of things—none of them innocent.

When he didn't respond she continued. "He's been here for over an hour and when I said I didn't know if you'd be in, he said he'd wait."

"No problem." Cobra's generic answer had her mashing her lips together, but being a savvy woman she swallowed her comments.

Some of the guys had been against Cobra's decision to put Patrice in charge, but she'd excelled beyond Cobra's expectations. She was tough, smart, professional with the customers, and able to keep the twenty dancers they employed in line. Not an easy job to appease women who made thousands a week and were constantly vying for the spotlight. The security team of muscle-head bouncers kept the peace, and Patrice kept the money pouring in.

Cobra sipped at his whiskey as he weaved his way to where Vinnie sat alone, totally uninterested in the action around him or the half-dressed girls gyrating on stage.

"Ahhh Cobra, sit down." Vinnie probably tagged him the

minute he walked in, but acted surprised. Another form of bullshit this man loved so much.

Cobra slid into the chair, never breaking Vinnie's gaze. "What're ya doing here?"

"Sipping some of this premium bourbon." Vinnie held up his glass. "Fine liquor for a strip club."

Cobra kept his face expressionless. Vinnie never stopped digging, always hoping to hit an open wound. Ecstasy equaled Sapphire or Treasures or any of the high-end strip clubs in Vegas and Vinnie knew it.

"Again, what the fuck are you doing here?"

"Always so crude, just like that other friend of yours, Joker."

Joker's new wife, Daisy, involved Vinnie using one of his porn studios in the desert for a scam that went a tad south. As in a dead body, numerous suspects and a raid from the Metro police orchestrated by Vinnie, but the Serpents proved once again they could make shit happen. When it came to the Metro Police, the Serpents and Vinnie Black were equals.

Cobra shot his whiskey, slammed the glass down, then placed his palms on the table to stand. "I don't have time for bullshit."

"Then I'll take up my problem with your manager, Patrice. Maybe she can explain how my weekly stipend has been short all month."

The Serpents owned Ecstasy and they ran two weekly poker games out of the backroom, and yeah, Vinnie took a cut. When they'd first opened, they needed his investment. He'd called it a gentlemen's agreement. Only one problem. Vinnie was no gentleman, and that bill had been paid a long fuckin' time ago.

Cobra smoothed his hands over the polished wood table,

eyes fixed on Vinnie. "You weren't shorted, you're just getting what you deserve."

"Hmmm, an odd comment for someone who needed my help back in the day."

"Maybe you oughta cut back on your wardrobe budget." Cobra's eyes roamed over his perfectly tailored suit.

Vinnie's grip tightened around his glass. "Always the smartass."

"I'm thinking since this arrangement isn't working anymore it's time to dissolve our partnership."

Vinnie studied him with cold emotion. "That could be risky, especially with Metro looking to make examples out of their less desirable citizens."

"I think I already proved who has the power with Metro."

Vinnie's eyes narrowed, remembering his latest failed attempt to screw with Cobra.

"You certainly do enjoy all the perks. Motorcycles, sports cars, that high rise penthouse." Vinnie's gaze flicked to Patrice standing at the end of the bar. "Do you think an exquisite woman like her would even give you a second look if you didn't own this club? A woman like that needs special attention."

Cobra pulled out his cigarettes, knocked one out of the pack, and lit up.

"And if you can't pay up what you owe, maybe I'll just have to take this establishment back."

"Try it." Cobra dragged deep and huffed out the smoke. "And all you'll have is an empty room 'cause without my guys running security and Patrice running the girls this place would fold within a week."

"Oh, I think I could persuade Patrice to stay." His snake-like lips curled.

Cobra and Patrice had an on-again, off-again business/fuck buddy relationship. Probably not healthy, definitely not professional, but Cobra had no illusions about Patrice. When the dust settled she'd follow the money. It was one of the things he liked about her.

"Let's stop screwin' around," Cobra ground out, tiring of this game of cat and mouse. "You're not interested in taking over, and I'm done paying you. So let's cut our losses and move on."

"Memory is a funny thing." Vinnie paused and looked off to the side like his next words would bring world peace. "Some events fade away, while others remain crystal clear. Like the day you called me after your first clubhouse burned to the ground. Ranting and raving about the rival gang you were sure did the job." Vinnie drew in a deep breath. "I still remember that drive out I-15 and the turnoff on that deserted road. Boiling hot that day, but I got the job done, and now you act like none of that matters." He touched his chest. "It hurts."

If Vinnie ever tired of being a first-rate scumbag he might try acting 'cause this performance was stage worthy.

"You better watch out Vinnie you're starting to sound like a bitch."

Vinnie's eyes bulged seconds before he slammed his glass to the floor. Shards of glass exploded against the laminate flooring, and the people around them stared until Vinnie pinned them with an evil glare. "I want my money." His voice low and smooth, his breathing controlled and even.

Two bouncers flanked Cobra as a waitress scurried around removing the broken glass.

"You're bleeding." Vinnie offered Cobra a cocktail napkin. "I abhor violence, but sometimes it's the only way to make a point."

Cobra wiped at the blood on his check from the broken

glass, then reached for his cigarette, but it burned out. He pulled another out of the pack, stuck it between his lips and Vinnie lit it. Cobra drew deep, letting the nicotine seep into his bloodstream. His right hand twitched and the reaction pissed him off.

Vinnie pushed away from the table and stood. "Many people say the mob is no longer in Vegas." He leaned over the table only inches from Cobra's ear. "Don't believe them."

"You need anything, boss?" The bouncer fussed around him handing him another napkin for his face.

Cobra waved him away. "Get the hell away from me."

The deep bass of the music pounded inside Cobra's head, leaving little space for rational thoughts. The familiar ache in his chest made it hard to breathe and the thudding of his heart warned him of what was to come. He needed to get out of the club, he needed air, anything to ward off the wave of dread, and loss of control.

Patrice stepped in his path and he moved around her.

"What happened?" She grabbed his forearm. "Where are you going?"

He pulled away from her, not able to take a full breath, his head buzzing. "I gotta go." He bolted to the exit as she called after him. He barged through the double doors surprising the bouncers on the other side.

"You all right, boss?"

He stormed into the parking lot, sucked in a lung full of dry air, then realized he'd parked his bike in the back. When he reached the side of the building he stopped and leaned against the brick wall as a cold sweat covered his arms. He braced his hands against his knees as his heart tried to pump its way out of his chest. His uneven gasps made him light-headed, his stomach clenched and for a split second he thought he would puke or faint. He forced himself to pace his breathing. In and out until his heart slowed. Drained and covered in sweat, his strength and breathing slowly returned to normal.

"Fuck," he muttered, massaging his temples, then cracking his neck on each side. He hadn't had one that bad in a long time.

No matter how many ways he tried to fight against them, the panic attacks always won. Sex, booze, even some premium drugs didn't work. He found out the hard way that most street drugs actually made them worse.

He pushed off the wall and raked his fingers through his hair as he ran through his choices for the rest of the night. Patrice would gladly try to ease his pain. Either in her second-floor apartment over the club or right there in his office. She'd made it clear that she wanted him for herself, and he'd taken advantage of that, but a relationship with her was too complicated.

Getting serious with the manager of one of the Serpent's biggest moneymakers was not smart. Who the fuck was he kidding? It had nothing to do with being smart. He didn't know the first thing about a real relationship. And yeah, that made him a dick, but he'd never promised her a future or anything else.

He dug his hand into his jeans and pulled out his cigarettes, then patted his pockets for his lighter. Shit! He must've left it in the club. He trudged toward the door not willing to leave behind the red Zippo lighter with the cobra design on the front. Danny's last gift to him before the accident.

He pushed past the people waiting for the bathrooms, and one of the bouncers approached him holding up the lighter. "I figured you'd be back for it."

Paying people a little extra always assured their loyalty. That and knowing if they fucked up they'd be out on their ass. The bouncer returned to his post by the bar, Cobra paused, and stepped into the shadows.

There at the end of the bar sat Vinnie and Patrice, their heads close in deep conversation. Cobra examined their body language. At one point, Patrice became animated, waving her hands around, but Vinnie remained his cool, detached self. Interesting.

Cobra watched them for a few more minutes, then left the club and made his way to his bike—His one salvation. Riding cleared his head, but he was still too amped up to go home. Without thinking he ended up outside the Gold Mine again.

At 1:00am the place would be crowded enough for him to lose himself. One of the newer prospects nodded and opened the door for him as some others roamed around in the parking lot keeping eyes on the bikes. The smell of smoke, beer and bodies calmed his jangled nerves. Joker and Daisy had left and some of the topless girls were now giving lap dances. The place was in full swing and he loved it. Ecstasy was the money shot, but the Gold Mine was home. He'd sit at his table in the back and relax. No bullshit, no drama just—Shit, she was still here.

Sheena stood at the very end of the bar, exactly where he'd left her. Alone and focused on the tiny shot glass in front of her. He'd assumed she would've gone tailing after that guy, Seth. He even had visions of the dirty shit they might be up to by now, but instead she was here looking just as fuckin' hot as she did two hours ago.

The last thing he needed tonight was another woman in his life, or another woman hung up on another guy. More aggravation, more drama and the absolute worst idea ever.

CHAPTER THREE

The minute Cobra entered the Gold Mine Sheena knew it. The air stilled, and the whole dynamics shifted. Yet, when she looked around nothing had changed. Guys at the bar, or playing pool, topless girls dancing to the hard rock music blaring out of the speakers. Couples making out in corners. No one else seemed to experience this metamorphoses but her.

Her position at the service bar allowed her to watch him swagger in like he owned the place. Oh right, he did. Or the Serpents did or some such. Daisy and Joker tried to explain the whole biker culture to her over the last month, but it seemed like an odd lifestyle. Strange thought coming from a con artist and scammer. Well, former con artist and scammer.

After the debacle in Miami with the cartel, her, Daisy, and Seth swore off all cons and scams. Dressing up every night in a pirate costume and slinging drinks to tourists at the Pirate Cove, a theme bar on the Strip, might be boring as hell, but at least she knew she'd wake up every morning to see another day.

The one good thing that came out of that whole mess was

Daisy found Joker, and although he had some rough edges he loved her and she loved him. Sheena's sincere joy for her best friend stirred some unfamiliar feelings of her own. Feelings that she didn't understand or like. The main reason Sheena fled to Vegas five years ago centered around independence and freedom, so thoughts of companionship rocked her.

Independence kept her sane and while men were a welcomed diversion they'd never been the main act. So how scary that the crystal blue eyes and movie star face of a man she barely knew made her stomach twist and her chest ache.

She stared down at the empty shot glass in front of her and decided to blame these ridiculous feelings on tequila. Yes, the root of all evil actions—Liquor. She shifted slightly to get a better view of this mystical man that turned her brain to mush, but he'd disappeared. After her brief brain freeze into retrospection, she'd lost sight of him. Here one minute, gone the next. She glanced at the shot glass. She was way over her limit so maybe her tequila-soaked brain was playing tricks on her.

Great. Most people saw double when drunk, not a hot biker with a body that—

"So, what are you still doin' here?" Sheena startled as Cobra tapped his finger next to her shot glass. Her gaze traveled up his arm and over his magnificent biceps, landing on his lips as they twisted into an antagonizing smirk. "Thought you were switching to water."

She turned too quickly, and almost lost her footing. Their hips butted together like an awkward dance move, and when his hand shot out to steady her it came in direct contact with her ass. Her eyes went wide when he kept it there longer than necessary.

"I thought you were leaving for the night." She quickly recovered, but couldn't mask the slurring of her words.

"What was that you said, 'Have a nice life.' Like we were never going to see each other again." She filled her glass and raised it. "Here's to pleasant surprises." The word pleasant came out like peasant, and he smiled.

"I think that's the first time I've seen you smile." She leaned into him. "You have a great smile."

"Never been told that before."

"Oh c'mon, you have to know how good looking you are." She waved the shot glass around spilling some of its contents on the bar.

"Or maybe I just don't smile that much."

"Well, you should. The first time I saw you I almost creamed my panties." She clamped her hand over her mouth. "Shit, did I really just say that?"

Cobra flashed that magnificent smile again. "I think it's time to get you outta here." He motioned to Rattler behind the bar. "Get me the keys to the SUV."

Sheena gripped the edge of the bar. The floor and the walls started moving against her will. She leaned into him like she was going to reveal a big secret. "I don't think I should drive."

"No shit." He cocked his head and the light shone against his serpent earring. "I'm taking you home."

"I don't wanna leave yet," she protested.

Rattler slid the keys in front of him and he put his arm around her waist. "C'mon, time to go before you barf on your shoes."

She rested her head on his shoulder and wailed. "Nooooooo."

Rattler gave him a little salute on the other side of the bar. "Good luck with that, boss."

Joker's firm hold around her waist didn't stop the floor from shifting under her feet. Like some Coney Island funhouse where every step took total concentration. He steered her out of the bar to a huge black SUV and she dug her heels into the pavement.

"I wanna ride on your bike."

"Not tonight, babe." He tweaked the locks and opened the passenger door.

She pushed against him. "C'mon, you're a biker, you've gotta have a motorcycle."

Cobra nudged her toward the open door. "We wouldn't get out of this lot before your ass would be hitting the black-top." He half lifted, half pushed her into the passenger seat. Then he pulled the seatbelt across her and locked it in place.

She leaned into him, practically pushing her breasts into his face. "Such a gentleman."

He slammed the door, got in on the driver's side, and started the engine. "Where do you live?"

"Right off Flamingo."

"What street?"

"Victor, no Viking." He shot her a look that said, you don't know where you live.

He motioned to her purse. "Take out your driver's license."

"It has my old address. After Daisy moved out I got a smaller place. I just moved in a few days ago and . . ." She rubbed at her forehead as if that would improve her alcohol drenched brain. "It's right around the corner from a bank and a CVS."

"That narrows it down." Cobra deadpanned, then spun into a gas station, around the pumps and out the other side. "Too late for a scavenger hunt. I'll take you to my place and hopefully your memory will return in the morning."

"I guess that's okay since Daisy's my friend and Joker's your friend, so that makes us friends too, right?" She twisted in the seatbelt to face him. "It's good to have friends. Do you wanna be my friend?"

"Sure." He chuckled. It was a nice sound.

"I normally don't drink this much. I know everybody says that, but it's true. When Daisy and I would run cons the object would be to get the other person drunk while we poured our drinks in the potted plants." She giggled, then hated that she giggled. "I think I drank so much because of Daisy getting married. Everything's changing and I'm going to miss her, you know?"

"She's not going anywhere." They stopped at a light and Cobra turned his baby blues on her. "You'll still be friends."

"You have the lightest eyes I've ever seen." Sheena knew she was staring, but she couldn't seem to control her mind or her mouth. Damn tequila.

Cobra headed to the other side of the Strip, then south on I-15. "So, when did you move to Vegas?"

"What makes you think I'm not a native."

"With that New York accent, no way."

"What accent? It's you that has the accent. And it's New Jersey, not New York."

"Same thing."

"No, we New Jerseyites are very proud and we don't like being lumped in with New York all the time."

"Sorry." He made a goofy face and she laughed.

"New Jersey is very unique. We're known for Bruce Springsteen, Bon Jovi, diners, going down the shore and—"

"Gangsters?"

"What?" Her alcohol haze cleared enough for her to be suspicious.

"You know, The Soprano's."

"Right." The streetlights filtered through the windows and her mind wandered to New Jersey. A different time, a different place, and a different identity. "I ran away," she blurted, then wanted to shove the words back into her mouth.

"From a guy?"

Running from a controlling guy would've been easy compared to what she'd been up against.

"Not exactly." Their eyes met and his quiet observation made her want to reveal all her secrets. Come clean with all the shit that came before Vegas. Things she hadn't even told Daisy. Secrets that could still destroy her, but instead she clamped her jaw together fearing what might come out. Damn alcohol made her stupid. Not good.

After passing the airport, Cobra took the next exit and weaved his way down a street dotted with high-rise apartment buildings.

When he pulled the SUV into a driveway with a sign reading Vegas Towers she turned to him. "You live here?"

He hopped out of the truck and tossed the keys to the valet, then came around to her side as she fumbled with the seatbelt. He released the strap and helped her out of the vehicle, then slammed the door. He wrapped his arm around her waist and led her into an enormous marble-floored lobby. She knew she wasn't firing on all cylinders, but something was way off here.

"Aren't you supposed to live in some grungy clubhouse that stinks of stale beer and piss?"

He laughed out loud as he ushered her onto the elevator and slipped a keycard into the slot, causing the door to whoosh closed. She swayed with the slight movement and his hold on her tightened. A few seconds later the door slid open into a wide corridor. He guided her down the carpeted hallway, then slipped the same keycard into a massive door.

He nudged her into the foyer and her eyes widened. "I'm totally confused. We're not breaking and entering, right?

COBRA STARED at Sheena as they stood in his foyer. When she swayed into him on the elevator he'd let his hand stray below her waist. A dick move, but he'd had a shitty night and the feel of her lush hips under his palm sure did improve his mood.

She was so wasted that he was able to take her all in without worrying about being caught in the act. That guy Seth was definitely an asshole for letting her slip through his fingers. This girl had it all. Curvy body, wild, wavy hair and lightly tanned skin that made his fingers twitch just aching to reach out and touch what he knew would be smooth and flawless.

Best of all he liked her sass. Breaking and entering —Priceless.

"Why are you staring at me?" she slurred.

So much for not being caught in the act.

"Just enjoying the view."

And that was the damn truth. The minute he walked in the Gold Mine earlier he was drawn to her. Telling himself to ignore her and just head to his table alone was total bullshit. Who the hell did he think he was kidding? Of course, he went over to her.

Even he didn't understand the attraction. He knew nothing about her except that back in the day she and Daisy ran cons together. Not hard to believe with that spitfire attitude, but she knew nothing about biker life, or his position in that life.

He supposed in some lifestyles not knowing that much about each other would be exciting, but not in his world. In his world suspicion and doubt ruled out attraction or any normal feelings. He needed a woman who knew he couldn't talk about his life, knew he wouldn't be home every night, and was ready to roll with it. Not some mouthy chick that met him toe to toe.

Now, here they were standing in the foyer of his penthouse. Her drunk off her ass and him with a raging hard-on. Yeah, bad decisions and him were like an addict holding the pipe. Lethal, dangerous and out of control.

She staggered her way to the floor to ceiling windows overlooking the Strip. "Wow, great view."

"One of the reasons I bought the place." He moved beside her and she leaned into him. Her hip only inches from his painfully swollen dick. He better shut this down before his good sense took a nosedive right off his twentieth-floor balcony.

She spun around suddenly, faltered, and touched his cheek. "What happened to your face?"

He covered her hand with his. "Got too close to a snake."

She furrowed her brow, but didn't ask. Then she wrapped her arms around his neck, molding her body against him. Staring at him with those huge, ebony eyes she leaned up, and parted those pouty fuck me lips that shot off all those smartass comments. He cupped her ass and goddamn if she didn't grind against him while her tongue swept past his lips. Her sweet mouth made love to his, and for a few minutes he forgot he was trying to do the right thing.

Her hand slipped between them and she palmed his raging cock. His hips moved without his permission and she rubbed harder. Ahhh, fuck me, was this some kind of test? Some punishment for all the shit he'd done in his life, 'cause this was goddamn torture.

She shifted her body and he gripped her ass tighter, as his eyes searched for any flat surface. The couch, the table, shit, he'd screw her against the wall or right here on the hard

before him while he lounged on his massive oak bed. He lifted his hand and his snake ringed fingers waved her forward.

"Let's see if it's worth letting you live." His full lips twisted into a smirky sneer.

She inched her way closer and his smile grew wider. He folded his arms behind his head and she froze. Redemption and Sacrifice were etched in ink on the underside of his forearms.

Sheena bolted upright in bed. Panic flooded her senses as her eyes locked on the grey and white streamlined furniture, soft bedsheets and large floor to ceiling windows covered with retractable blinds. Definitely not a rogue pirate's bedchamber or her tiny room on Viceroy Street. Thinking of her street name recalled a shadowy memory from last night.

She followed the buzzing until her eyes locked on her phone in the semi-dark room. She lifted the annoying object and read the screen. Daisy. Shouldn't she be snuggled up in bed with Joker. Finally, the screen went black and the damn thing stopped buzzing.

She examined herself, rumpled but still fully dressed, and tried to put the last twelve hours together in some kind of order. Drinking at the Gold Mine alone and then with Cobra. Driving with him in a car. No, an SUV. He'd taken her here to what must be his apartment.

She heard muted voices in the next room so she eased off the bed. The room dipped and spun one way while her stomach rolled another way. She leaned on the bedside table and sucked in deep breaths to ward off the overcoming nausea.

Her tongue stuck to the roof of her mouth and her eyes stung like she'd spent the last twenty-four hours staring at the sun. Random, disjointed thoughts flickered through her feeble brain and she cursed the makers of tequila. How could any human beings produce and distribute such a lethal substance?

When her stomach settled she stumbled to the en suite bathroom. Keeping the offensive lights off, she ran the cold water and splashed her face until it was numb. Slowly raising her head she ventured a peek into the huge mirror over the sink while raising the dimmer on the light switch. She was reminded of those before and after shots in magazines. She was either the way before, or the long after.

Her naturally tawny skin had taken on a yellowish tint and her eyes were hooded with bags big enough for a trip to Asia. Her hair was an entirely different story. Normally, she loved the wild, thick, curliness but this morning its unruliness couldn't be tamed. No amount of hair product, or heat could fix this craziness. Not good. Not good at all.

She turned away from the mirror, to save her tender stomach anymore distress. She couldn't hide in this room all day, yet the alternative of facing Cobra and whoever he was talking to—Shit, how did a smart, savvy girl get herself into this predicament? Tequila, right.

"I HOPE Cobra realizes how lucky he is to have a beautiful woman in his kitchen cooking." Python leaned over Patrice by the stove. "Pancakes, my favorite."

Patrice plated four pancakes, doused them with syrup and handed it to Python, then jerked her chin at Cobra. "Mr. No-Carbs doesn't eat pancakes."

Cobra drummed his fingers against the quartz counter-top. He'd told Python he'd meet him downstairs, but of course knowing it was Sunday and knowing Patrice would be cooking breakfast he showed up early. A fact Cobra conveniently forgot while nursing his sex hangover for Sheena.

"Well I eat everything." Python cut the pancakes, stabbed them with his fork and shoved some into his mouth.

"So I've heard." Patrice waggled her eyebrows.

"Ahh darlin,' you've been talking to Fiona."

Cobra contemplated pouring syrup over Python's head. This was exactly what he wanted to avoid, especially with Sheena still sacked out in his guest room. And no, he hadn't told Patrice yet. Getting caught in between the woman he was screwing and the woman he wished he —Fuck yeah, he was a dog and a coward.

The faster he got Python out of there the better. He'd seen the six-foot-four, two-hundred-and-fifty-pound giant beat down their most lethal enemies, but the man loved gossip. He could sit and dish it faster and better than any of the women at the clubhouse. Cobra didn't want to think about what all he'd have to say about Sheena sleeping it off in his guest room.

"I'd like to get the hell outta here." Cobra glared at Python, then shot a look toward the guest room door hoping to get gone before Sheena made her inevitable entrance. Okay, not the best plan. Not even a plan. More like a man trying to save his ass anyway he knew how.

Python slung his arm over Patrice's shoulders. "You can come cook for me anytime, babe."

"Let's go before you embarrass yourself." Cobra grabbed for Python's plate, but he managed to fork up more pancakes before giving it over.

"Too late." Python threw his fork in the sink, then leaned into Patrice. "You ever get tired of his grumpy ass, you come see me."

Patrice smiled sweetly at Python, then nailed Cobra with

a pointed look. "I have a few errands to run, but I'll be back later." She rinsed Python's plate in the sink. "How long will you be?"

The woman loved to ask questions she knew he couldn't answer. "As long as it takes." Of course he could always ask about her chatting up Vinnie last night, but he wouldn't give her the satisfaction. This arrangement was definitely on the way out.

"That's clear as mud." Sarcasm and Patrice was like peanut butter and jelly. A boring combination.

"You know the drill, babe." Cobra loved to egg her on.

"Right, the mysterious biker with all your secretive errands." The smirk on her face told him she loved this verbal volleyball. Why the fuck, he had no idea.

"We're still on for tonight, right?"

"Right." Unless you go into the guest room for some reason and see the hot brunette laid out on the bed.

Cobra pushed Python toward the door and then onto the elevator. The door whooshed closed and Python nailed Cobra with a look. "Who pissed on your shoes this morning?"

"Don't." Cobra hoped the one word would convey his mood.

"What?" Python attempting innocence was like a bear walking a tightrope. Impossible and hard to watch.

"Just shut it."

"For fucks sake I was eating pancakes. And just for the record you really oughta treat a hot piece like Patrice a little better. Shit, the way you were rushing me outta there you would've thought that you had—"

The door opened into the lobby and Cobra bolted past Python. "You parked out front?"

"Whoa. Wait one mutherfuckin' minute." Python said to Cobra's back.

Cobra exited the building and hopped into the passenger seat of the late model Ford truck. Less conspicuous than Harley pipes blasting through the desert.

Python joined him in the driver's seat, stuck the key in the ignition and turned to him. "You, me and Patrice weren't the only ones in the penthouse, were we?"

The engine turned over and the heavy motor chugged to life. "Shit brother, I'm impressed. Two women in one night in the same apartment." Python grabbed for the pack of cigarettes on the dashboard. "Remember Monica that used to work at the Chick-fil-A over on Sunrise? She had a friend and the two of them used get off and then get me—"

Cobra slammed his hand against the console. "Would you please shut the ever-loving fuck up."

"C'mon, man, at least fill me in on all the details. It's a long ass ride out to the desert."

"I got nothing to say."

"For a man who got his dick wet all night you sure are pissy."

They remained silent until they hit I-15 and Python slammed his hand against the steering wheel. "It was Daisy's friend, Sheena, huh?"

Cobra's deep sigh sent Python into a fit of laughter.

"Not that it's any of your damn business, but nothing happened last night."

Python threw his hands up, then gripped the steering wheel again. "You had two hot ass women in your place and you didn't screw either of them."

"It wasn't like that; Patrice just came by this morning. She doesn't even know—"

"Holy shit, so you got Patrice in your kitchen cooking you breakfast and you got Sheena holed up in your room."

"For your information, she's in the guest room, and I'm not interested in your comments or your opinions."

"Fine, so I won't point out that Sheena isn't one of us and you shouldn't get involved with her because she probably wouldn't get the life. Or that Patrice is a crafty bitch who's only love is money and if you piss her off she'd sell you out to Vinnie in a fast minute."

Cobra glared, hating that Python just spit out the truth.

"I'm done." Python tapped his rings against the steering wheel. "Why are we making this trip again? We were just out here on Thursday."

"Vinnie claims he's got some new workers he wants me to check out."

"New workers? What the hell was wrong with the old ones?"

"Who knows. Let's just get there, check it out and get gone."

"Right, I'd feel the same way if I lived in a place with hot and cold running women."

"Very funny." Cobra flipped him off. "But you don't know what you're talking about."

"I know that Patrice isn't into sharing and I also know that she's got Vinnie's ear, and he may not like it when she's unhappy."

"I don't give a fuck what he likes."

"Sure, that's why we're driving an hour out into the desert and an hour back to check out something we just saw three days ago," Python deadpanned.

Cobra cut a look to Python. His oldest friend and sergeant at arms was the only one who got away with giving him shit. Then he gazed out at the barren, rocky landscape whipping past them on I-15. He'd drank just enough last night to be left with a gnawing headache, and an edgy uneasiness about what they would find in the desert.

The large trailers scattered all over the Southern Nevada desert that housed hundreds of illegal marijuana plants brought in a big profit. A headache free business where they hired locals to tend the plants, paid them for their discretion and everybody left happy. They even had a few grandmothers who gave the plants tender loving care.

Cobra and Python drove out every two weeks. They brought back product, handed it over to Vinnie for distribution and everybody got a percentage. Easy, simple. Now, Vinnie claimed that this change would double their profits. Cobra was all about the money, but why fuck with perfection?

"I'm in his guest room," Sheena whispered into the phone.

"So just leave," Daisy whispered. "Why am I whispering?"

"I can't, there's another woman in the kitchen."

"Oh my God, you did a threesome?"

"Nooo," Sheena hissed into the phone. "She wasn't here last night." Although there were parts of last night that were a black hole. But no—She certainly would've remembered a menage a trois, right?"

"Who is it?" Daisy asked.

"I don't know." Sheena inched the door open just enough to see a tall brunette's reflection in the huge mirror of the hall. Her willowy thinness made Sheena hate her on site. Okay, that wasn't nice but she could hate her for keeping her captive in this guest room. "She's cleaning up the kitchen."

"Maybe Cobra has a cleaning service."

"Believe me, this is no cleaning woman." Sheena opened the door an inch more for a better look. "Definitely not the cleaning woman."

"Well, you have two choices. Stay locked in the guest room, or be your usual badass self and go out there and introduce yourself."

Daisy was right. When did she ever retreat from an uncomfortable situation? But Cobra had taken care of her last night and if this was his girlfriend she'd never believe that something didn't happen.

"Sheena?"

She glanced at the phone screen. "I'm running out of power. Don't worry I'll figure something out." She swiped the phone and when she peeked out the door again the kitchen was empty. She listened to the quiet for a few minutes, then inched the door open. A few minutes later she edged out into the hallway. Silence. She crept over the carpet like a cartoon character waiting for a bomb to explode in her face. She made it to the foyer when she heard a noise. Not waiting or wanting to find out who or what it was, she turned the door handle and bolted.

CHAPTER FIVE

Cobra massaged his temples willing the ache to disappear. He waited for the rest of the Serpents to drop their phones in the box by the door, file into the back room of the Gold Mine and take their place around the table. The small room was just big enough for the long, oak table and ten chairs for the patched members. They weren't as big as some of the other Nevada chapters, but then they only took care of what went on in Las Vegas, while some of the other, bigger chapters controlled larger portions of the state.

He rotated his neck as the guys ribbed each other with the usual bullshit.

"Sit the hell down," Cobra growled. "I ain't interested in who you fucked last night, or how many you fucked last night. Let's get this going."

"Shit, boss." Rattler dropped his large frame into the chair to Cobra's left. "What crawled up your ass?"

Cobra pinned him with an evil glare that sent Rattler searching his pockets for his smokes.

Sensing his mood, the others quietly stared at him. Normally, they razzed the shit out of each other, and normally, Cobra didn't call church on a weekend, but after their trip to the desert, he was in no mood for jokes.

Cobra cleared his throat, and leaned in. "I think we all agree that this club is about making money."

Fuck yeah and *hell yeah* echoed around the room.

"And that we have no problem bending the law to make that money."

The ten men around him nodded.

"But what Python and I saw today goes beyond bending the law." He paused and a few of the guys exchanged looks. "Vinnie's replaced most of our workers with Asian women. Underage Asian women. From what I could understand from the men overseeing them, they're here against their will. Slave labor."

"Shit, that ain't right." Boa lit up a smoke, shaking his head. As treasurer of the club, he handled the money and even he wasn't willing to step in this shit.

"It gets better," Python added. "The guy we spoke to had a heavy accent, but from what I got, Vinnie's also using these girls for his porn business."

"Vinnie's nothing if not efficient." Cobra spat out, then cracked his neck hoping to relieve the tension that had accumulated since they pulled away from those trailers.

"He just does this without a sit down." Rattler stubbed out his cigarette in the dented metal ashtray. "That fucker is getting a little ahead of himself. Shit can't get any worse than that."

Cobra drummed his fingers on the wood table. "So you'd think."

Heads jerked in his direction. "What else?" Rattler asked.

"Along with the weed, he thought it would be a good idea to bring in bootleg fentanyl patches. According to the guy that's handling these girls, it calms them down, makes them more willing to do porn."

"Ahhh, hell no." Rattler shook his head. The rest of the guys mumbled their disgust.

Comments flew around the room with the guys getting loud until Python waved his hand around and roared, "Shut the fuck up, and let's figure this out."

"Growing illegal weed is a category E felony, at worst a year in the joint." Cobra said.

Weed was basically legal in the great State of Nevada, but you had to get a license to sell it, and that license had a long ass waiting time, a high price tag, and an intricate vetting system. In short, outlaw bikers with records would not be granted a license. Plus, you had to pay taxes to the state for every sale made which cut way into the profits.

"Possession of fentanyl gets you twenty years." Cobra crossed his arms on the table top. "Human trafficking is a federal offense, puts us in a shit load of trouble, and it's a dirty fuckin' business. I got nothing against porn or the people that make the flicks, but drugging and forcing underage girls ain't right. Turns my stomach."

They all mumbled their agreement.

Boa pounded his balled fist onto the table. "We don't work for Vinnie, we work together. Our deals with him are supposed to be a partnership, not some fuckin' dictatorship."

"What I can't believe is that he just went and did this shit." Rattler lit up another smoke.

"What the hell does Vinnie care? We're the ones on the ground doing all the legwork, while he sits around the Bellagio entertaining his high rollers for his next big stakes game." Python tapped his fingers restlessly against the table. A sure sign he was ready to blow.

"We've always run this shit like a business, so maybe the workers should go on strike," Rattler offered.

"Exactly what I was thinking." Cobra turned an evil smile on Rattler. "All those shit hole games he runs in backrooms, warehouses and basements attract the lowlifes banned from the casinos. Money, booze, weed and psychos can be a lethal mix, and with no security who knows what could happen."

Python cracked his knuckles. As the club's enforcer, he headed security, vetted and organized all the bouncers at the strip club and the games. His massive muscles were always primed, and since he'd never liked Vinnie he was ready for a fight.

"And don't forget his biggest game over at that warehouse on Valley View." Python smirked. "Every dealer and pit boss plays there cause they're not allowed to play in their own clubs. A hit there would put a dent in that fuckers profits."

They all fell silent. Going over the plan in their heads.

"The only place we keep security is at Ecstasy. Can't leave the girls hanging high and dry with a roomful of horny bastards jerking off." Python turned to Cobra. "That way you don't have to worry about Patrice."

Cobra guessed it should've been him thinking about Patrice, but business had been his only thought. Another indication that their relationship was tanking and it was time to get out. When he hadn't heard from her earlier, he assumed that she hadn't caught Sheena in the guest room. Good because he wasn't in the mood to deal with her bullshit, bad because it would've set him free.

He'd been with plenty of the girls at the club before Patrice. No commitment, nothing serious. He'd always been up front about it. No games, no tricks. When it was time to move on—he moved.

Patrice would be different though. Her shrewdness and smarts set her apart from the others. When it came to what she wanted she was single-minded and she never gave up without a fight. An asset when running a business like Ecstasy, a big headache when trying to ditch out of a relationship.

"Right, boss?" Rattler asked.

Cobra shot a look around the room realizing he'd zoned out for a minute.

"I'll give the bouncers the word tomorrow," Python repeated. "Then I'll make sure the word gets around to the right people that Vinnie's games will be unprotected."

"Sounds good," Cobra said. "Can't wait to hear from the big man when shit starts happening and he's left holding his dick."

CHAPTER SIX

"So, you just ran out of there, and she never saw you?" Daisy asked.

Sheena plopped down on the sofa at Daisy and Joker's new condo down in Henderson. "Crazy, but it was the least I could do. After all, he did take care of my drunk ass, and he was pretty nice. At least the parts I remember." Sheena held her head. "I haven't been that drunk since—ever. It was just such a weird night. Celebrating your wedding, then things not working out with Seth. I don't know." She blew out a long breath. "He has the most extraordinary eyes."

"Seth?"

"Cobra. They're like icy blue, so light and . . . they sparkle. I mean it's like they're lit from within." She paused. "Why are you staring at me?"

"I've just never heard that tone in your voice. I mean, no offense but you usually go through guys kinda quickly. And now you sound almost dreamy."

Sheena raised her eyes to the ceiling. "Dreamy… really? I don't think so."

"Got a thing for the hot biker with the sparkly eyes?"

"Hardly." A memory of him carrying her into the guest room last night flashed through her brain. Tatted biceps and —words etched on his forearms that she couldn't remember.

"Right, I'll believe you if you tell me what you were just thinking about."

Daisy knew her so well.

"Shouldn't you be on your honeymoon?"

"Fine, don't admit it," Daisy said. "And we're waiting a while until Joker gets the motorcycle shop up and running. We're a little short on money right now."

"I can relate to that, but I'm sure you don't feel like listening to me complain about my money problems." Sheena finished off her wine. "You don't need me here crying in my wine when your new husband gets home."

"It's fine." Daisy waved her off. "Anyway he won't be home for another hour." Daisy refilled her glass. "Continue."

"The bottom line is, I don't make enough money."

"Who does?" Daisy sipped at her wine.

"I've downsized to a smaller place, I've cut out extras like clothes I don't need, wine I shouldn't drink, but not the makeup. I positively need and love my makeup." She sighed deeply. "I guess I got too used to the good life, and working at the Pirate's Cove is definitely not the good life. The tips suck and the little salary I make gets lost in the taxes."

"And that good life could've landed all our asses in jail or worse. Main reason we adopted the straight life."

A bad con in Miami ended with a dead body, and two hundred thousand dollars missing. They weren't responsible for the corpse, but the two hundred thousand was never found.

Sheena's head told her Daisy was right, but . . . "Straight life, huh? More like boring as shit life with no room for advancement and no money."

"Better than a lifetime sentence in Ely State Pen," Daisy reminded her.

"You're right, I'll just have to find another job." Sadly that was easier said than done. Although she changed her name legally, paranoia set in about her past.

"A legit job." Daisy used her mama bear voice.

Sheena hated deceiving her best friend, but a girl had to survive and if dealing some poker at underground games run by Vinnie Black spelled survival, then break out the cards.

———————

THEY ENTERED THE SOLARIUM, and Cobra pushed Danny's wheelchair right up to the expansive window. He pulled a chair over to sit next to him. Danny's face light up at the sight of the ducks and swans that swam in the man-made pond.

Chronologically, Danny was twenty, and after extensive therapy he understood everything you said, but he could only respond in short sentences. The beating their father had given him ten years ago left him with brain damage and a severed spinal cord, paralyzing him from the waist down.

In the dead of night, the sound of his brother's moans, haunted him. Crumpled up on the linoleum floor of their crappy trailer like a wounded animal caught in a trap. Cobra enlisted specialists, and therapists to help Danny, but in the end there was nothing they could do. He was destined to be strapped in a wheelchair. A prisoner in his own body.

The extravagant cost of Danny's care and rehab drove Cobra to Vinnie. The Serpents were just starting out and Vinnie needed some inside guys to run the weed farms. Back in the day, it made sense. Vinnie fronted the money and the Serpents did the leg work and the security at the poker games. By the time Vinnie invested in Ecstasy Cobra's future was set. He'd sold his soul and made his deal with the devil.

Cobra reached out and squeezed Danny's hand to draw his attention away from the wildlife on the other side of the glass.

Danny stared at him. "You're sad."

Cobra smiled at his perception. Even as a kid he was sensitive to everything and everyone around him. They might've shared blood but beyond that they were total opposites, which was why their bully of a father constantly rode Danny.

"No, I'm good." Cobra forced a smile.

Danny shook his head, his expression somber.

"Okay, you're right, as always. Got some stuff going on at the club. Nothing to worry about, just bullshit."

"More."

"Yeah, more." Cobra mashed his lips together. "Met this girl and I can't get her outta my head, but she's all wrong for me. I'm not feeling it with Patrice anymore, and I don't know how to get out of it." Cobra pulled a goofy face. "Women. Can't live with them, can't live without them."

"Heartbroken."

Another rueful smile tugged at Cobra's lips. You had to have a heart to have it broken and Cobra was sure there was nothing as fragile as a heart inside his chest. The almighty powers of the universe had taken care of that detail, yet he kept fighting. Surviving.

At an early age he'd learned to duck to avoid a fist, or make himself invisible when dishes and cups went flying against the wall. Then everything changed. He grew taller and stronger and the hate and anger inside him grew too, until it consumed him and molded him into an empty shell.

He owned a mirror and he knew what others saw on the

outside. Sure, he'd managed to glean the best from his dysfunctional parents. Height and strength from his drunk, survivalist father and penetrating, crystal blue eyes from his heroin addicted mother. Getting women had never been a problem, but keeping them was another story because sooner or later they learned that he had nothing to give. An attractive package, and once the wrapping was pulled off there was nothing but empty box.

The only place he felt whole and worthy was straddling his Harley, zipping down a desert road or weaving in and out of a crowded highway. The anguish vanished with the sound of the pipes, and the roar of the engine. Nothing compared to that except—Sheena.

He didn't even know her, yet something about her tugged at him. A cagey wariness like she too was hiding some deep, dark secret. His secrets were abstract where hers seemed more tangible, real and maybe even dangerous. Sheena's layers were complicated.

Danny squeezed his hand bringing him to the present. "You, okay?"

"Yeah buddy, I'm fine." Cobra reached into his pocket. "Geez, I almost forgot." He handed Danny a packet of Topps baseball cards. The kid had books and books of plastic covered collectors cards. He read every baseball magazine and never missed a game on TV.

Danny painstakingly pulled away the foil wrapping. It wrecked Cobra to see his slow, deliberate movements, but Danny was proud and wanted to do it himself. He cast the wrapper aside and carefully shuffled through the cards examining each one.

He raised his head and their identical eyes met. "Thank you." The thick, emotional timbre of his voice almost broke Cobra. Paralyzed from the waist down with a brain that didn't work right and he was thankful. Fuck, but his kid brother had more balls than him or any of his outlaw bikers.

Cobra's throat tightened and he swallowed hard, then he leaned in and hugged this special human being. How his messed-up parents had made someone so perfect was beyond his comprehension. His brother's thin arms couldn't make it around Cobra's bulk, but he savored the closeness of the only pure thing in his life.

Cobra straightened and squeezed Danny's shoulder. "See you tomorrow."

Danny smiled, then raised his hands like he was throttling a motorcycle.

"Don't worry, you'll hear me leaving." Cobra squeezed his shoulder one more time, then headed toward the door.

One of the aides stopped him in the hall on his way out. "Danny so looks forward to your visits. You're such a good brother."

If she only knew the truth.

CHAPTER SEVEN

Sheena hadn't exactly lied to Daisy about getting a job. It just wasn't the legit job she'd led Daisy to believe. Since Daisy moved in with Joker, Sheena had to get another apartment in North Las Vegas. Not a great part of town, but all she could afford.

She'd gotten used to luxury. She'd grown up with it, and then when that was ripped away she'd fled to Vegas. For the last four months she'd tried to play it straight, but pulling cons was exciting and so very lucrative. Yes, she knew it was wrong, but her larceny came naturally. A screwed up DNA inherited from her mobster father.

After another grueling night at the Pirate's Cove, Sheena's mind was made up. She'd swallow her pride and corner Seth at the end of his shift. Since the night at the Gold Mine they hadn't talked, but it's hard to ignore someone on the same shift wearing the same ridiculous pirate costume. Usually, she either beat it out of the Pirate's Cove or lagged behind cleaning imaginary spots off the bar, but tonight she waited by Seth's luxury SUV.

He approached with a wary expression, so she forged ahead once he got in earshot.

"I need to ask you a favor." Her voice sounded stilted, and it saddened her how their relationship as friends had suffered.

"Sure." He leaned against the SUV.

"Nice truck." She motioned to the Escalade. "But I know you don't afford it working here."

His brow furrowed. "The tips here are good and—"

"The tips here suck and the pay is even worse. Don't bull-shit a bullshitter."

Seth had worked at all the big clubs on the Strip until the eye in the sky caught him double dealing.

"I want you to tell me how you afforded this vehicle. Or better I'll tell you how you can afford it."

"What do you want, Sheena?"

"You're dealing for Vinnie, right?"

He gave away nothing. The perfect con with the poker face. No pun intended.

"I'd like you to get me in again. Regardless of what happened or didn't happen between us, you have to admit I was one of the best."

They'd worked in unison, a perfect pair, then things got weird. She'd taken their work relationship to mean more. Obviously she'd been wrong.

"Are you still with that biker?"

Why did he have to bring Cobra up? Didn't he know that she was trying her best to forget how he pulled her off the dance floor the very night she met him. No questions asked. How his commanding presence fired up her adrenaline. The scruff on his jaw and the hard glint in his eyes said edgy and dangerous while his angular features and crystal blue gaze said Hollywood. Yikes, she had to concentrate.

"Not what we're talking about."

"You want back in the game?" He frowned. "I thought you liked playing it straight."

"I also like eating, and this place," she motioned toward the bar. "is barely paying my rent."

He blew out a heavy sigh.

"I'm not asking for a kidney. I've worked for Vinnie before, just get me a sit-down with him. I'll take it from there." She shrugged. "Easy, and you're done."

"All right, I'll do it, but that guy Cobra is trouble and you should definitely stay away from him."

"Thank you for your unsolicited advice." She tried to ignore his comment only because she refused to admit Seth was right. Cobra was trouble, a seductive inconvenience wrapped in a sinful body that made her senses sizzle and her mind short circuit. Yeah, that wasn't helpful.

THE NEXT NIGHT Sheena met Vinnie at the Bellagio casino bar. The notorious "fixer" of all things illegal was decked out in a designer suit, and although he was average height, he definitely made a presence.

She slid into the seat next to him. He nursed either a whiskey or a scotch, but never asked her what she wanted which was fine. She wanted to remain sharp and professional for this exchange. Who knew interviewing to cheat people at cards could be so stressful. The thought made her smile and he caught her.

"A joke I'm missing?" His narrowed eyes trained on her.

"Just thinking that . . . Never mind. You were saying."

"With your skills I never understood why you gave it all up."

Of course he wouldn't. The man oozed corruption, and made a fine living because of it.

"Seth highly recommended you and of course I know about your skills first hand."

Of course, he knew, in the old days she'd played a big part in his profits. Plus, by definition it was his job to know about people. How else could he 'fix' things if he didn't.

"And because you and Seth have worked together before, I want you to work together again."

"Oh, I don't think that'll work. You see—"

"Maybe I left out the most important part of this job description." Vinnie's face flattened, void of all emotion. Like reptiles that had no body temperature. "I tell you how this will go down and you do it."

His low, even tone rocked her with its menacing under-current. Her head nodded without her permission, as if under a spell of hypnosis.

"Have you forgotten all the things I know about you or the way those things would change your life here in Vegas?"

Sheena swallowed hard. He had her right where he wanted her.

"As I was saying, you and Seth will work together at the table. You'll be the dealer. Women dealers are always the most advantageous. Since most of my customers are men, and traditionally men are stupid creatures when it comes to beautiful women . . . they're easily distracted. Seth will be introduced as just another player. And I don't suppose I have to tell you how the rest of the evening will play out."

Nope, he didn't. The old been there, done that was never truer. She'd run many cons, but the easiest was the collusion scam.

Sheena would deal from the bottom, middle and top of the deck. Sometimes Seth would win, sometimes he would lose.

No one would suspect because it was subtle. Sheena charming the other players and Seth playing the role of regular guy, but in the end Seth would be the big winner raking in all the chips.

Then after the game broke up, Seth's winnings, were divided amongst them. Vinnie, of course getting the highest cut. Every game Vinnie ran had a shill, and they were always nondescript everyday guys like Seth who liked to play poker.

"I'm also assuming you and Seth have your own ways of communicating."

"You assume correctly."

"You'll start tomorrow night. I'll text you the address, and then of course you'll delete that text."

"Of course."

Vinnie turned to the bar and his watered-down drink. She waited for half a minute until she realized their meeting was over and she was dismissed. She'd also wanted to mention that this arrangement was short term, until she could get some money together. That she didn't want this to be permanent, but Vinnie made himself clear. This would go down the way he wanted for as long as he wanted.

Sheena walked out through the casino with a jittery sensation. Not because she was working with Seth, or because she'd be back in the game. That all came second nature, like brushing her teeth or combing her hair. No, her bout of nerves came from whom she'd be working for. A man so icy cold that nothing penetrated. Scary at best, deadly at worst.

"So, what do you think of the place?" Cobra waved his arm over the expanse of Ecstasy's main room.

"It's a strip club, man." Joker glanced around the low-lit room. "You've seen one, you've seen them—"

"Nah, this place is all class." Cobra loudly cut Joker off, pointing to the tiny lights that illuminated the stage, then to the ornate brass railing that kept the guys far enough away from the dancers. He made sure his movements were broad, and clumsy and his voice rose just enough over the music. Let the eyes that watched him see a guy with just a little too much to drink.

They'd settled at Cobra's usual spot just off to the side of the stage. Close enough to see all the action, but far enough away from the speakers to be able to talk. Cobra attempted to kick his foot up on the table, but missed.

Joker laughed, then slapped his friend on the back. "You're right, all class."

Cobra pulled out a pack of cigarettes, offered one to Joker and when he leaned in to light up, Joker said, "Which one is Vinnie?"

"The only asshole in here wearing a designer suit." Cobra sucked in a deep drag. "Last table by the service bar," he said, perfectly sober.

Clarissa, one of the headliners circled their table then leaned in to Joker. "Hey baby, want a private party?"

"He's a newlywed." Cobra laughed.

"Doesn't bother me, if it doesn't bother him." Clarissa shoved her fake tits in Joker's face.

Joker pulled out some cash and angled himself toward her hip. "Not tonight, babe." He stuffed the money in her g-string while surveying Vinnie at the back of the room. Smooth move. They came off as just two guys screwin' around in a strip club. Now if only he could convince Joker to be his VP.

Cobra slapped his hand on the table. "I knew Daisy had your balls in a vise."

Clarissa laughed with them.

"Like I said, my buddy here just got hitched. Permanent pussy deserves a celebration." He waved his hand over the table. "More shots."

"Coming right up." Clarissa wiggled her way to the bar.

The music changed and the announcer introduced another dancer. A new girl with waist length blond hair wearing a white, lacy teddy exposing her ass and barely covering her tits.

Patrice returned with the shots, placed them on the table, then leaned in and kissed Cobra's cheek. "Hey, sweetie."

Cobra cocked an eyebrow. "Waiting tables now?"

"Only for our VIP customers." Her smile was stiff and fake. "How're you tonight, baby?"

"Doin' good." Cobra knocked back his tequila.

Tension shaded her face. "There's another VIP customer by the service bar."

"I noticed." Cobra's fist clenched on the table top.

Patrice held his gaze like she was waiting for him to say more. Some guys wound their way behind her trying to get a table closer to the stage.

"Good crowd tonight." Patrice leaned into Cobra's ear and he could feel Vinnie's eyes on them. "Anything particular you want me to tell him?"

"Not a thing." Cobra deadpanned. His mind flickered to her and Vinnie the other night, and just how much she might be telling him. She straightened, and Cobra caught her eyes flick over his shoulder seconds before she extended her perfectly manicured hand to Joker. "I'm Patrice."

Cobra waved his hand in her direction. "She keeps the place running smooth."

"Nice." Joker flashed his trademark smirk.

"Shall I send over Clarissa for your friend?" Patrice asked.

"She already stopped by." Cobra measured his words. "We're good."

Patrice didn't miss a thing that happened in the club, so all this small talk didn't add up.

"I'll come check on you later," Patrice ground out, her eyes hard.

Joker's eyes followed Patrice until she blended into the crowd. "If you're trying to hit that, I suggest you work a little harder."

Cobra ashed his smoke, then dragged deep. "She likes it when I act like a dick."

"Then she must love you." Joker shot the tequila.

"It's complicated."

"That's a whole lotta complicated." Joker barked out a laugh. "She's the type that could make you light yourself on fire."

"Fuck, if I don't know it."

Joker sank against the upholstered seat and threw his arm over the back of the booth. "I understand you took Sheena home the other night."

How'd you find out?"

Joker plastered a huge grin on his face. "Daisy and her are best friends, and women can't keep shit to themselves."

"You're worse than Python." Cobra rubbed his hand over his stubble. "Nothing happened."

Not that he hadn't thought about it, not that he hadn't wanted it. It freaked him the fuck out how many times he'd pictured her over the last few days. The smell of her hair, the feel of her hips against his palm. She'd popped into his brain when he should've been concentrating on business or when he was riding, or any time at all. Fuckin' crazy.

Joker shrugged. "Don't matter to me, I ain't your priest."

"Fuck you."

It bugged him that Joker figured him out. With most of the women it was one and done. Even his pseudo relationship with Patrice was nothing permanent. Although she seemed to think so.

"Ohhh shit, I knew you had it bad for her. I could tell the way you were looking at her the other night." Joker knocked his knuckles against the table, then pointed at him. "And now it's pissing you off that nothing did happen."

"You don't know nothing."

"Right, that's why just talking about her has your fists all balled up."

Cobra sliced his eyes to the table. Shit, the annoying fucker was right. He relaxed his hands, and reminded himself where his head should be tonight. Not on some sexy brunette with a hotter than hell body.

Cobra motioned to Joker's tequila. "Take your shot and shut up."

The spotlight changed color as the next dancer hit the stage, and for a split-second Cobra's eyes connected with Vinnie's.

Tonight was all show. Tonight was about being seen. Tonight was about being right under Vinnie's nose. Front and center and innocent as fuck.

Joker slid his chair closer to Cobra, and glued his eyes to the redhead on stage. "When's it all going down?"

Cobra cut his eyes to his phone on the table reading the time. "Another fifteen minutes. Then every five minutes till they hit all five places. Twenty-five minutes is all I need to show that bastard who's boss."

Cobra let word slip to the Desert Rats, a rival MC, that Vinnie's five biggest games would be without security.

"By the time he realizes what's going down it'll be too late," Joker said.

Vinnie had cut the DR's out of a deal last year, and Cobra knew they would jump at the chance to get back at the slimy bastard. The Desert Rats were famous for smash and grabs and if some of Vinnie's loyal workers got roughed up in the process—Nothing like broken bones to send a message.

Cobra raised his shot glass with a crooked grin for Vinnie's sake. "Exactly."

"Couldn't happen to a better fuckin' person." Joker pointed his cigarette toward the stage like he was commenting on the dancer.

Joker had his own reasons for hating Vinnie. Like trying to sucker Daisy into his illegal shit, then hitting on her and being an all-around douche. Vinnie knew how to piss people off.

Cobra grinned. "We saved the biggest heist for last. A warehouse over on Valley View. Usually attracts casino middle management looking to blow off steam. Since they can't gamble in their own casinos, Vinnie offers an alternative. Plenty of cash on the table, booze, women and no regulations. The best part is the DR's are jacking him up and giving us a cut. So it's a double fuck you."

Cobra faced the dancer on stage while his eyes wandered to Vinnie at the back of the club. Maybe a loss of revenue would wake the big man up.

CHAPTER EIGHT

Sheena parked on the side of the low-lying building. She expected some dark shady entrance, but the whole parking lot including the entrance was well illuminated. She guessed the kickbacks Vinnie donated to the police department every month insured his protection from those pesky raids that made Metro so famous.

She easily found the metal stairs that led to a large industrial door. The kind with the huge handle that was almost impossible to release. Inside rows of low pallets stacked with boxes were marked with different auto parts. Knowing Vinnie he probably had his hand in the rampant car theft that plagued the city. Not her concern. She was here to deal cards, nothing else.

She made her way down the widest row of pallets as Vinnie had instructed and found another door. The lack of security surprised her, but she chalked it up to Vinnie's arrogance that no one would dare mess with him.

She opened this door and did the cliched double take. Like stepping into Alice's Wonderland, this space resembled a cross between a downtown loft in Greenwich Village and a new age club on the Strip. Somehow the cement floors and the brick walls meshed with the black leather banquets, and chrome railings. No sliding fake walls or fold up tables here. This room screamed permanent location.

Within the confines of the relatively small room Vinnie packed in two craps tables, two roulette tables, a few slot machines against the wall and the one and only poker table where she would deal.

Most people would never suspect that illegal gambling could prosper in a town where legal gambling reigned supreme but they'd be wrong. Take one huge city already stocked with gamblers and add in tax free winnings, no limit betting, and no vetting for the high rollers with criminal records who'd been banned from the legal casinos.

Mix them up with a guy who has his hand in the pocket of the Metro police, connections to gamblers all over Vegas and Macao and you have the Vinnie Black Underground Gambling Show. Vinnie rarely made an appearance. He just sat in his literal ivory tower at the Bellagio counting his coins. Biggest business within a business.

Sheena spotted Seth at the bar talking with one of the pit bosses that ran the table games and the manager. Most of these guys were professionals who lost their jobs at the real casinos because they'd palmed too many chips. No chance of that here. Vinnie was manic about security, vetted his players and kept close watch on the staff. Who better to pick out a cheater, than another cheater?

Although tonight security was almost non-existent. Strange and a bit scary considering some of the clientele.

The players were starting to take their seats at the table and Sheena joined them. No need to be social, this was a job. Seth would be to her right in the lead-off position. Basically regulating and raising the stakes to keep the other players in the game. Of course, they didn't know that. With all the people Vinnie had working for him it was a simple task to rotate people so the players never caught on.

Seth sat and smiled like they were pleasant strangers, not weird friends who had so many stops and starts Sheena lost count. As everyone situated themselves around the table Sheena discreetly leaned into Seth.

"Not much security here tonight." She let her eyes wander the room. Bouncers were a much-needed asset when half the players were shady characters and the money circulating in one night could buy a small tropical island. She'd literally walked right in so what was to stop some thug looking for a big heist to do the same.

———

COBRA AND JOKER continued their act of two guys in a strip club, knocking back shots and drinking beers. They kept the conversation going, talking about bullshit, and every few minutes Cobra let his eyes stray to Vinnie nursing his scotch.

"Still need a VP." Cobra threw out the offer again.

Joker lit up another cigarette and dragged deep. "Told ya before, not interested."

"Sure could use you." Cobra sipped at his beer. "Especially now."

"I'll help you with when you need, but I don't want no fuckin' titles. I gotta think about Daisy and Derek. Can't get deep in that shit anymore."

Cobra respected a man who put his family first.

And finally it happened. Through the loud music, colored lights and smoky haze Cobra saw Vinnie pick up his phone. Vinnie hunched over the table, then his back stiffened, but when he pounded his fist on the table Cobra smiled. All the signs of an egomaniac getting fucked in the ass.

Cobra leaned into Joker. "Looks like the first hit just went down."

Joker raised his glass and they clinked them together in a toast. "Fuck with me and I fuck you worse."

"Abso-fuckin-lutely."

Whoever said revenge wasn't sweet didn't know Vinnie Black 'cause right now Cobra felt like the king of the goddamn universe. He had Python and the rest of the guys keeping a lookout to make sure everything went down smooth. Oh yeah, they'd be doing some heavy duty celebrating at the Gold Mine tonight.

When his phone lit up with a call from Rattler, Cobra smiled.

"Hey brother, give me the good news."

"Those fuckin' DR's don't disappoint. They charged into that body shop on Bonanza and messed it up good. I went in with one of the prospects when they were done and that place was fucked up. A few of the players got slashed, probably trying to play hero. One of the dealers got a busted head. Nothing too serious, just enough to send a message."

"All right. Make sure the DR's meet up with us at the Gold Mine later. I want that money divided up right, and then we'll show them how the Serpents party."

"You got it, Prez. See you later."

Cobra was just about to tell Joker the good news when his phone lit up again. This time with Python. Oh yeah, this was turning into a good fuckin' night.

"Cobra?"

"Tell me how the DR's are tearing Vinnie's shit up." Cobra knocked a cigarette out of the pack and stuck it between his teeth.

"Cobra, listen to me."

The tone of Python's voice made Cobra grip the lighter tighter.

"I'm over on Valley View, and the DR's aren't here yet, but I thought you'd wanna know—"

"Sit tight, I just heard from Rattler. They fucked up the place on Bonanza and should be headed to you soon."

"No man, listen. Your girl Sheena just walked into the warehouse."

"What the hell is she doin' there?" Sweat popped out on the back of his neck despite the heavy-duty air-conditioning.

"Fuck if I know. What do you want me to do?" Python asked.

"I'm on my way."

Cobra stood and shot a look to the back table. Vinnie was gone.

"What's up?" Joker asked.

"I gotta get over to Valley View. Some shit going down."

Joker stood with him. "Let's hit it."

Two questions jumped around Cobra's brain. What the hell was Sheena doing at Vinnie's warehouse on Valley View, and could he get there in time?

COBRA HOPPED off his bike flanked by Joker. The industrial area consisted of big box warehouses illuminated by halogen security lights casting eerie shadows over the silent parking lot. Python stood at the far end of the parking lot his eyes wary and waiting for direction.

"They just went in." Python nodded to the bikes parked closer to the warehouse with the Desert Rats insignia.

"You sure it's Sheena in there?" Last thing Cobra wanted

to do was barge in and screw up a perfect heist. Especially on Vinnie's biggest earner.

"I'm sure. I've had eyes on the place for over an hour. That guy Seth is in there too."

"That pussy isn't going to do anything to save either one of them." Cobra raked his hand through his hair. "Can't just leave her in there swinging. The DR's are a bunch of fuckin' animals."

Cobra turned toward the warehouse and Python pulled him back. "You think this is smart? Maybe she's working for Vinnie. Like maybe her coming on to you the other night, getting into your penthouse was all a scam. A way to get info."

Python's words made him pause. He wouldn't put anything past Vinnie, and he had just met her.

"You don't even know her," Python added. "She could have her own angle."

Fuckin' Python, always in his head. It was like the man could read his mind, but he was right. This hit would mess with Vinnie's bottom line, and this warehouse raked in the highest profits. Was he throwing that all away for a woman he barely knew and might be scamming him?

A slow burn simmered in Cobra's chest. Sure, Sheena was drunk off her ass that first night at the Gold Mine, and acted all messed up and vulnerable, but he hadn't actually seen her drink that much, and maybe her ignoring him and that whole scene with Seth was a con. Plus, he'd left her alone at his place the next morning.

"I don't think so," Joker chimed in. "Her and Daisy have been friends for a few years."

"And you told us both of them ran cons for Vinnie so—"

"No fuckin' way," Cobra cut Python off mainly because

he couldn't admit that maybe Python was right. Was she back in the game? And was he the target?

"If we go busting in there it'll screw up our deal with the DR's." Python rolled on the balls of his feet. "Us showing up will be a lack of faith," Python added.

Didn't matter. It was one thing to let the Rats do a smash and grab on Vinnie's games, but they had some shady reps when it came to women and he didn't need anything else crowding his conscience.

Cobra's thoughts were interrupted by a loud boom and then gunfire.

"You coming with me or not?" Cobra barked.

"I'm with you." Python's expression said 'you're my president and I gotta follow you, but you're making a huge mistake.'

As they barreled through the warehouse, they heard loud voices and general mayhem. Cobra banged into the private room with Python and Joker on either side of him.

One of the Rats had the players corralled against the wall. Two other Rats had the pit bosses stuffing cash from the tables into bags while Seth, Sheena's jealous ex, dumped the cash from the poker table into another bag.

Cobra's pulse amped up. That stupid bastard probably got her involved in this shit show or they were in on it together as Python suggested. Fuck, what the hell had he gotten himself into?

Cobra stepped further into the room and spied a fourth guy in the corner of the room hunched in front of a safe with the door hanging at an odd angle. Must've been the sound they heard. Blew the door right off of it. The Rats didn't fuck around.

Cobra scanned the room again, but no sign of Sheena. Python seldom made mistakes, so where the hell was she?

Demon, the President of the Desert Rats whirled around to face them. The metal from his multiple face piercings glinted against the lights, and his glassy eyes shone, as he pressed a gun into Sheena's side. A familiar sense of dread surged through Cobra. His blood pumped hot through his veins. The room shrunk to Sheena, and the gun.

Demon smiled wide like he wasn't holding a woman at gunpoint. "Come to check to make sure we got the job done?" His voice high-pitched and tight.

Python leaned in. "He's fuckin' spun."

No surprise there. The Rats were high on something all day every day. The same thing that made them perfect for this job, also made them extremely dangerous now.

"No man, we got faith." Cobra motioned to Sheena. "But the girl ain't part of it."

"I know, but she sure is a nice reward for a job well done." Demon wiggled his tongue, then licked the side of Sheena's neck, pressing the gun further into her side. "I'm just keeping this here so she don't run away."

Cobra locked eyes with Sheena. Fuckin' impressive. Her expression remained blank, her body still, reserved, but ready to pounce.

Cobra advanced a few steps keeping his voice conversational. "We're gonna party later at the Gold Mine. All the bitches you want." He waved his hand at Sheena. "Why waste your time on one when you can have your pick later."

Cobra could see Demon's messed up brain processing, but he kept the gun tight to Sheena's ribs. Joker and Python edged closer. He trusted the skills of both men, but one slip and a bullet would be imbedded into Sheena's side.

He cut a glance to Python, then to Joker as all three men did a silent countdown. One would disarm Demon, one would get Sheena safely away and the other would clean up the mess.

"Hands up, drop your weapons," a voice boomed from behind him.

Cobra spun around to see four Metro cops in the doorway. Two of the Rats fired on the cops and when Demon raised his gun Cobra lunged and yanked Sheena away from him. The Demon's returned fire along with some of the players. Guys scattered, people screamed and the smell of gunfire filled the small room. Nothing like being caught between a renegade MC, the cops, and gamblers who had nothing to lose.

Python upended a poker table and pushed him and Sheena to the back of the room as Joker covered them. Cobra shielded Sheena with his body as gunfire blazed around them. More tables overturned and he used them for cover as he made his way to another door.

Instead of surrendering to the cops the crazy ass Demons and some of the gamblers were fighting in a blaze of gunfire.

"Go, go, go," Python pointed to a door at the back end of the room.

Sheena stumbled and Cobra wrapped his arm around her waist, and lifted her off her feet, carrying her like a football to the end zone. Her feet dangled at an odd angle and if the room didn't stink of gunfire and bullets weren't zinging around them it might've been funny.

"Keep going. Out that door," Joker yelled through the chaos.

Bullets splintered the wall in front of them, but Cobra kept running dragging Sheena with him, making sure that his body covered hers. He pushed through the door with Joker and Python close behind him. Python slammed the door, then wedged a nearby hand truck under the handle.

They all paused to regroup, and Cobra loosened his grip on Sheena's waist so she could stand.

"Guns popping like a fuckin' video game," Python huffed out around a harsh laugh. "Crazy mutherfuckers shooting it out like an old time western."

Cobra surveyed the smaller open space.

"Looks like a loading dock." Joker pulled on the heavy chain until the metal garage-like door slid open. They jumped the few feet to the ground, then ran to their bikes. Luckily, the cops were parked on the other side of the large rectangular building.

"Head back to the Gold Mine like nothing happened," Cobra told Python as he shoved his gun into the waist of his jeans. "If the cops show up, deny you were here, and say you don't know nothing. It all went down so fast, they got no proof who was there and who wasn't."

Cobra turned to Joker. "Thanks for the help in there." They did a handshake backslap thing. "You sure do act like a VP."

"Hard to break old habits." Joker mounted his bike.

Python jerked his chin in Sheena's direction. "What are you gonna do about her?"

"I'll meet up with you at the Gold Mine later." Not the answer Python wanted, but Cobra had some things to figure out first.

Python glared for a minute too long, then sped off on his bike.

Cobra reached out to Sheena. "Are you all right?" She seemed fine, no blood, no bruises.

"I'm fine." She swung her leg over the seat of his Harley. "Let's get out of here."

He paused for a second, jolted by her calm, then hopped on his bike and kicked it to life. As they roared out of the warehouse parking lot he checked his rearview mirror, but nobody followed them.

Cobra's brain spun with questions. Questions he'd make her answer once they were safe. Questions for which he might not like the answers. She'd had a gun stuck in her side by a spun out tweaker, narrowly escaped getting arrested or shot and held it all together. Impressive, but he wasn't stupid. That was not the normal reaction of a civilian, male or female.

Sure she ran cons, but that made you savvy, not tough. Not saying a woman couldn't hold it together, but you only got that way from experience and living the life. Which made him wonder, what was her backstory and how many fuckin' times had she been held at gunpoint? Even the toughest women in the club would be shook with a .45 sticking them in the ribs. He'd love to say that she was ride or die all the way, but something didn't mesh. Something didn't add up.

CHAPTER NINE

Sheena held tight to Cobra as he gunned the engine and rocketed out of the warehouse lot. So many questions whirled around her head about how the night went down, but seeing Cobra there blew her away.

The thug that Cobra referred to as Demon was a straight up psycho. Clearly strung out on something, but Cobra's sheer presence and don't fuck with me attitude—Impressive. As they whizzed through the Vegas streets she looked over her shoulder a few times, but thankfully no one followed them.

The night could've easily ended differently. Like in the back of a police van or an ambulance with a bullet lodged in a major organ, but thanks to Cobra they'd made it out unharmed. Maybe what they said about certain events in your life happening to prepare you was true. Thanks to her past she was able to keep it together, not fall apart, and react when Cobra rushed Demon. Running cons helped with her acting ability, but the grit in her blood was inherited, for sure.

She forced herself to relax and let the warm air surround her. Held at gunpoint, hiding in safe rooms, witnessing bloodshed, typical Jersey Girl, yet she'd never been on a motorcycle. The smell of gasoline, exhaust and Cobra's enticing maleness.

She liked being hugged up tight against his broad, muscular back. His thin, black t-shirt showcased every plane and ripple of his sculpted body, and Sheena marveled at how well they fit together. She also noticed the outline of the gun shoved into the waist of his jeans. He'd used that gun to save and protect her tonight. Like two renegades riding off into the sunset. But one question gnawed at her, how did he know what was going down, and what was he even doing there tonight?

Shit, then it hit her. Her dream. Cobra was the pirate who saved her. The swashbuckling, smirking renegade whisking her to safety, and his bedroom. Okay, so it was more like an outlaw biker and a scamming card mechanic running for their freakin' lives, but this was her dream fantasy and damn it, she'd spin it anyway she wanted.

Her fingers were having a little fantasy too as they gripped his firm abs. They flexed and twisted every time he shifted or turned the bike. Her mind traveled to what lay a few inches lower.

Cobra stayed off the Strip and all the major roads. She rested her head on his shoulder and enjoyed the dark, star-studded sky overhead. When he pulled into the garage of his building, a niggling disappointment slithered through her. He parked the bike, and cut the engine. She reluctantly unwound her arms from around his waist and stepped off the mighty machine.

He stared at her for a second longer than normal, then wordlessly guided her to the elevator in the garage and they rode to his floor. She tried to read him, but his face gave nothing away. A useful trait for an outlaw biker who probably spent most of his life either breaking or running from the law. Another similarity they shared.

The elevator door whooshed open and he placed his large hand on the small of her back guiding her down the corridor to his penthouse. His firm hold on her reminded her that he'd want answers. Answers she wasn't ready to give up.

Inside was as impressive as she remembered. The view, the furniture, the glass and chrome bar—and the same question gnawed at her. This was not the home of a typical outlaw biker. At least not the ones on her Netflix series.

Lost in her daydream, she startled when he slammed her into his rock-hard chest. A little whoof of air escaped her lips and he grinned.

"You were badass back there." He lowered his head and attacked her lips. He took his fill, then broke away from her. "And I wanna know why?"

Her brow knitted together. "Why, what?"

"Why you held it together so well, why having a gun shoved in your gut didn't shake you, and why—"

She stiffened against his palms. "In your world a women can't be as tough as a man?" she challenged. Keep him off track. Derailed.

"Nah, I ain't falling for that equality shit. I've seen guys twice your size piss themselves at gunpoint. This has nothing to do with women versus men. This has to do with you knowing the life."

She tried to pull out of his hold but his hands locked at her waist. The last time they stood here she'd been blasted on tequila, but now her senses were sharp and on point.

"Why were you there tonight?" His beautiful blue eyes sharpened to points.

She squirmed again, and he pulled her tighter to him.

Their eyes close enough for him to tell if what came out of her mouth next was truth or bullshit.

"That's none of your business."

He threw his head back and barked out a laugh, then shook his head. "Really? That's how you wanna play this." His face clouded over and the outlaw biker appeared. "Cause the way I see it, I saved your life and those bullets popping off could've ended me or my guys, so yeah, it is my fuckin' business."

"You're right." Placating worked with most men. As long as you agreed with them they went on to the next subject.

"So, answer me. Why were you there tonight?"

But not this dangerous biker with the startling blue eyes.

She heaved out a sigh. "I was dealing the poker game."

"Okay, that opens up a hundred more questions. So why don't you just come clean or I'm gonna think that you're working for Vinnie Fuckin' Black and that coming here the other night acting drunk was a setup. And believe me, it don't matter that you're a woman. If you're running some kinda scam on me or spying for Vinnie it's not gonna end well for you."

"So, you saved me from one dirtbag, just to do the job yourself."

"Don't compare me to that fucker." He gripped her ass and squeezed until she yelped. "I want the truth and I want it now."

———

WHEN HE SQUEEZED her ass and she yelped it sent a bolt right to his cock. He was a sick fuck.

"Along with running scams back in the day I'm also a card mechanic." Her dark eyes shone like black stones shimmering under water. "You know what a card mechanic is, right?"

"Yeah, smart ass, I know what it is."

She glared at him. "I'm not a spy for Vinnie."

"But you work for him."

"No—Yes. I mean I did, then I didn't, but lately money's been tight. Probably not the best decision I've ever made, but it was an easy fix."

"And that fucker Seth hooked you up, right?"

"Again, yes and no. Seth deals for Vinnie, but I approached him. I asked him to get me back in."

"Okay, so you and Seth were working together. You were dealing and he was the shill."

Her eyes widened and he smirked. "I know all about Vinnie's crooked games, and how they work."

She shrugged. "Then those guys stormed in and started trashing the place."

"And that's it."

"There was something else." She cocked her head. "I noticed there wasn't the usual security. I mentioned it to Seth, and a few seconds later everything went to shit."

Of course it did, but he'd be keeping his connection with the DR's to himself. She was hot as hell, and yeah, he wanted to believe her, and even though he threatened her, women and children were off limits. Always. But she didn't know that and when he threw around his don't fuck with me attitude he usually got results.

"That explains why you were there, now tell me why having a gun pressed into your side didn't scare the shit outta you?"

She mashed her lips together and he realized that was one of her tells. What came next would be a diversion or smoke screen or anything to deflect and redirect the issue.

Her lips parted but instead of revealing all her truths she pressed her lips to his, tracing her tongue along the seam of his lips. She tasted sweet and hot, like those perfect steamy coffees at Starbucks.

He broke away and stared into her dark eyes. "Not gonna work, babe. I want answers."

Joker told him that the cons she and Daisy ran took place in board rooms or country clubs, and their weapons consisted of a gold pen or a black Amex card. Tonight was completely different, so how come she didn't even break down afterward. If anything she was as amped up as him.

She pushed closer melding their bodies. Her body surrounded him, made his head spin, but he fought it off. He pushed her away. He couldn't touch her and think straight.

"C'mon, tell me all your secrets. Tell me where that badass attitude came from."

"It came from the same place that makes me want you now." She ran her hands up his chest. "Makes me hope that you want me too."

Was she fuckin' kidding? Did he want her?

Five days ago, they stood in this exact spot only then he'd done the right thing and all that bullshit 'cause she was drunk. Yeah, he was a sinful, outlaw biker, but taking a woman drunk off her ass was for punks and guys who couldn't get sober pussy. So he held back, even though it damn near killed him.

Now, here she was again, in his arms, still hot as hell, still ready and oh so available. She'd answered most of his questions, and right now he didn't have the energy or the self-control. He had a beautiful woman in his arms, giving herself to him and, fuck yeah, he wanted her.

"You want this?" He leaned down, grabbed her thighs, and she hopped up and wrapped her legs around his waist.

"Ohhh, god, yes."

Shit, a shootout with the cops and a rival club, then escaping with a badass woman on the back of his bike—that was enough to get any outlaw hot and bothered. Although he had to admit that seeing Demon with his gun pressed up against her side messed with his gut.

He walked them to his bedroom, and she ground against him. "Fuck baby, don't make me drop you." She smiled and when she did it again he grabbed her ass and squeezed. "I think I'm gonna have to punish you for that."

"Please do," she taunted, and he knew he was a goner.

He kicked the door to his bedroom wider, then dropped her on the bed. She squealed, as she leaned up on her elbows with big, round eyes and parted lips. Oh yeah, this was happening.

He toed off his boots and crawled up the bed hovering over her, enjoying the view. His hands aching to dig into the wild tangle of dark curls that surrounded her face. He wanted it all. On her back, legs wide open, ankles wrapped around his neck, on her stomach with that fine ass in the air. He wanted his cock to explore every part of her, and he wanted his tongue to taste every inch.

She pulled her skimpy t-shirt over her head and his head spun. Just as he imagined, her tits were perfect, and when she unsnapped the front closure of her bra he hissed in a breath. Fuckin' amazing and now he needed to add something else to his list. Slide his dick between those luscious mounds and let her squeeze him until he blew.

She palmed his cock and he ripped at the button and zipper of his jeans, then leaned over to his nightstand. He yanked open the drawer, pulled out a strip of condoms and ripped one open. When he looked back at her she'd already shimmied out of her jeans.

"I've got a question for you?"

He motioned to his straining cock. "Now, you wanna ask questions?"

"Figure I have a good shot of getting an honest answer."

Shit, this woman was too much. "All right, what?"

"Why were you there tonight?"

Sure, he could give her a bullshit story, but why bother. "To save you."

Her eyes widened at his honesty, but when her lips parted he leaned in and took her mouth again. "You asked your question, and you got your answer," he said against her lips. "No more talking unless you're screaming out my name while telling me how good I'm making you feel."

He needed to taste her, unable to keep his tongue from exploring. Her hand slid over his cock and he pushed it away, afraid he would bust like a fuckin' teenager.

He slid the condom on and settled between her legs. "Gotta have you now, gonna be fast, gonna be hard the first time, but I promise you we got all night."

She guided him in and it was game over. He pushed his jeans lower and ground into her deeper. Shit, he'd been in such a hurry he was fuckin' with his pants around his knees like a goddamn kid.

She arched her back raising her hips, letting him go deeper. She gripped his shoulders, nails digging into the sinews of his muscles. He planted his palms on the mattress to steady himself. She raised herself higher and he drove deeper wanting her to have all of him, just like he wanted all of her.

Their movements were smooth, fluid, like they'd been doing this all their lives.

"You're amazing."

Her fingers wrapped around the nape of his neck and

when she pulled at his hair he hissed in a breath. Or was that her. He didn't know and he didn't care. As long as she kept moving under him, letting him go deep, freeing him from the burdens and bullshit that plagued his mind.

He slid his hand into those crazy curls and tugged. She bucked harder, then wrapped her legs around his waist and squeezed. "You are one hungry woman. Goddamn' hellcat." He panted between shallow breaths.

"You inspire me." She leaned up and traced her tongue over the Serpents tattoo that started on his chest and ended at the base of his neck. His body clenched at the smooth strokes of her tongue.

He slammed into her, not able to pace himself, out of control, falling deep and hard. Feeling something for the first time in a long time.

"Fuck, baby." His body collapsed against her, his face buried in her hair. Breathing deep, he pushed her hair aside and sucked deep on her neck. For some reason putting his mark on her became a priority. She may still have some secrets but she'd know who marked her.

He laid on top of her until his brain functioned enough to tell him that he was way too heavy for her. He slid to her side and snaked his hand between them. He hadn't felt this light in —ever. Sex with Patrice always had an underlying agenda. Payment for agreeing with a decision she made at Ecstasy. A reward for a grueling week. Their sex always had a backstory, always had a motive. A price to be paid or a credit earned.

But this was different—His brain stalled. Sheena had evaded his last question before, and initiated the sex. Nah, you couldn't fake that kind of passion. She may have fucked his brains out, but he was around enough bullshit to know what was real and what was fake. What he saw in her eyes and felt in her body was the real deal.

His sex-soaked brain drifted to his responsibilities. He should've checked in with Python. He should've done it the minute they got to his place, but he'd let her work him. Forget his responsibilities.

He grabbed his phone off the nightstand as she slid her hand down the length of their bodies. Her brow furrowed. "The sheets are wet." She raised her hand between them and the dim light made it hard to see what was on his hand.

He leaned over and flipped on the bedside lamp. "Fuck!"

CHAPTER TEN

C obra jackknifed to a sitting position, threw the phone on the bed, and pulled away the sheet to examine Sheena.

"Oh my god, it's blood." Sheena pointed to the blood-stained sheets, then to his leg and the fresh wound on the side of his thigh. "It's not me, it's you."

"Ahhh shit, must've caught a bullet." He pulled the bedding away from his leg.

Sheena leaned over his shoulder to get a better look. "Are you all right?"

"Just grazed me." He looked over his shoulder, their faces inches apart. "Gotta say you pressing those gorgeous tits up against my back is making it feel a whole lot better."

She swatted his shoulder. "Get in the bathroom so I can clean that up."

He rolled off the bed, grabbed up his t-shirt and pressed it against the wound.

Sheena busied herself in his pristine master bath. "Where's your first aid kit?"

"Under the sink." He limped into the bathroom and sat on the edge of the jacuzzi.

She opened up the plastic box, and examined its contents, pleased to see it had everything she would need. He watched as her hands moved efficiently, unrolling the gauze, cutting the tape and uncapping the antiseptic.

"I'll need a towel to clean out the wound first." She motioned to the perfectly folded white towels on the rack. "I'm sure you don't want me to use those."

He rummaged around under the sink and found a more used hand towel.

She wet the towel, then gently cleared away the blood. "I can't believe you didn't feel this."

"Adrenaline, I guess." He smirked up at her. "That beautiful body of yours had me in a trance."

She looked between them noticing their naked bodies. "I should go put something on."

He grabbed her hand. "Nah, this is every biker's wet dream. A naked nurse taking care of his bullet wound."

"You like being an outlaw, don't you?"

"Best thing ever."

She rolled her eyes. "Let me get it good and clean so I can make sure there's no bullet fragments. They can cause an infection once the skin starts to heal if you don't . . ." Her voice trailed off.

His eyes bored into her, willing her to say more, but she kept her attention on placing the gauze over his wound.

"I guess you're not gonna tell me how you know all about patching up bullet wounds either."

She let the statement hang between them, secured the last piece of tape, and raised her head. "And I guess you're not going to tell me why an outlaw biker lives in a penthouse in a

luxury building. Or who that woman was cooking you breakfast the other morning."

They stared at each other, opponents in an edgy game of
Truth or Dare.

"The woman's name is Patrice. She manages Ecstasy, the
strip club the Serpents own, and I live in a penthouse because
I grew up in a four hundred square foot trailer in the middle
of the fuckin' desert. The winters were freezing cold and the
summers were boiling hot. I'm not going to bore you with the
bullshit I called a life, but I swore if I ever got any money I
would live in a clean place with heat and air-conditioning and
hot and cold running water."

"You also have a thing for cleanliness." She waved her
hand around the bathroom. "A little on the OCD side."

"Maybe." He shrugged.

"No maybe, those towels look like they're hanging at
attention."

"All right, all right."

"And the other guys don't mind you have a place like
this."

"Nah, they love living over the Gold Mine. A flight of
stairs away from all the beer and liquor you can drink, women
in and out all night, every night. They think *I'm* crazy."

"From a guy's point of view, yeah, but I understand
wanting something more, wanting something different."

She pointed to the Ride Till I Die tatted across his lower
abs. "I have a feeling that has an interesting meaning."

"Got it a long time ago."

They locked eyes and when he didn't continue, she
motioned to this leg. "You should get back into bed."

He reached for her. "I like the sound of that." He pulled
her down on his good leg and captured her lips. His kissing

skills were over the top. So powerful that the familiar tingles shot through her stomach and below.

She broke away from him and stood. "You're impossible."

"Not what you were saying before, babe. Let me think. It was more like 'give me more, don't ever stop."

She swatted at his ass as he left the bathroom.

"Nice, hitting an injured man."

His phone buzzed, and he swiped at it. Sheena listened, knowing that if you listened to a conversation close enough you could almost make out who someone was talking to just by the pronouns they used and the inflection in their voice.

He hung up and she stared at him, thinking he might say who is was, but he returned her look with silence. Of course, he'd never divulge club business, but the conversation didn't seem to go that way. His answers were short, formal and while not friendly, they were cordial, like he was talking to an acquaintance, a neighbor or an ex-wife or a wife you wanted to be an ex-wife.

───────────

COBRA ENDED the call and placed the phone on the bedside table fully aware of Sheena's eyes on him. Willing him to tell her who called him, but Danny's nurses nightly report was one secret no one knew about and that was the way he intended to keep it.

Just like he was sure she had secrets she was keeping from him. The efficient way she took care of his wound. Not squeamish about the blood, not fumbling with the bandages. Just like at the warehouse, she was cool and in control. Intriguing, like she was born to the life.

Cobra remembered the call he never made to Python, then

dismissed it. If there'd been more trouble he would've heard by now.

"So are you a paramedic or something?"

"No." She motioned to the bed. "Let me change these sheets."

"I don't get you. We've just had mind-blowing, fuckin' out of our minds sex and you won't tell me how you know how to clean up a bullet wound."

She pulled at the stained sheets, head down, ignoring his statement.

"Hey." He reached out for her. "You don't have to do that."

"You can't leave them like this—And you did save my life tonight, and take a bullet." She bent over to pull the sheets away from the mattress.

"It's little more than a scratch." He ogled her ass. "And you bending over like that is payment enough." He pointed to his rigid erection. "Your fine ass got the fuckin' thing all worked up."

She straightened with the bundled sheets in her arms. "Is sex all you think about?"

"Not usually, but that position gives me ideas on how we can spend the rest of the night."

She rolled her eyes. "Where are your clean sheets?"

"I'll do that." He gathered the bundled sheets from her.

She tilted her head to look up at him and her dark eyes made him not care what made her tick or where they were headed. She challenged him as no other woman, her secrets should've sent up a red flag, but somehow they calmed him, made them equals. Deception and survival was the regular, the air that kept him alive.

"Are you hungry?" She'd been too nervous to eat before the game, but now her stomach rumbled.

He rolled the sheets up and threw them into the hamper, then flipped up his phone. "The place downstairs only stays open till midnight. I'll call out for something."

"Do you have anything in your fridge or are you the typical male with only beer, catsup and soda?"

"No, smart ass, I got more than beer and soda." He made a goofy face. "But I probably don't have anything worth eating either."

"Let's see. But first, lend me a t-shirt or something because I'm not parading around naked with all those windows."

"Babe, we're on the twentieth floor. Give the pigeons a thrill."

She put her hands on her fabulous hips. "I'm not budging until you give me something to throw on."

"You keep standing there like that and I'ma throw you down onto that mattress and put that fine ass in my face."

She held her ground until he rummaged through his dresser coming up with a Serpents t-shirt they had made a few years ago for the bike rally in Sturgis. Then he pulled out a pair of sweat pants for himself. He tossed her the shirt, and smiled when she dragged it over her head. The freakin' thing hit her knees.

"How tall are you?"

She drew herself up squaring her shoulders. "Five foot six. Why?"

"You look good in my shirt, even if it fits you like a dress. You're so tiny."

"Tiny?" Sheena described herself many ways, but the word tiny never entered her list of adjectives.

"Think about it babe, at six three I'm almost a foot taller than you."

"I've just always thought of myself as kind of, not fat, but not thin."

"You're not fat or thin, you're just right. Curvy hips and an ass that makes me wanna bite it. You got a bangin' body, babe, but to me you're petite."

Okay, so she'd just had hot, crazy sex with an outlaw biker who probably broke more laws and had a rap sheet as long as his sinful body, but he'd called her petite. Right now he could murder someone in front of her and she'd defend him to the end.

"Let's go see what's in that kitchen." She bounded toward the kitchen feeling like a super model. She'd never had a man so innocently make her feel so good. And yes, she knew she didn't need to be validated by what a man thought of her or her body, but it was the almost awkward way he'd told her that was so . . . uncharacteristically sweet.

Right, a six-foot-three, over two-hundred-pound, gun toting, law breaking, don't fuck with me biker—Sweet.

She opened up the Sub-Zero refrigerator and was pleasantly surprised. She could definitely do something with this. She pulled out the cherry tomatoes, half an onion and a jar of garlic. Then she held up the leftover chicken. "How old is this?"

"It's fine."

Probably bought and prepared by Patrice, his mystery strip club manager who also prepares breakfast. Sheena wondered what other services she performed and then blocked that destructive thought. What did it matter? She wasn't interested in anything permanent and she was sure he wasn't either.

Twenty minutes later, the sweet smell of garlic and onions

filled the kitchen, along with simmering tomatoes. She'd rummaged through his pantry and come up with some spices, walnuts and olive oil, and after putting them together in his state-of-the-art food processor she had a very tasty pesto sauce to add to the tomatoes, garlic and onion. She also found a box of rigatoni which she added to a pot that looked like it had never been used. Everything in his kitchen looked brand new and barely used.

After changing the sheets, Cobra sat in one of the chairs on the other side of the counter. His kitchen was spectacular and the island was huge with a cooktop that allowed her to cook while he observed from the other side of the counter.

"You're pretty talented."

"Thank you."

When his lips quirked into a smirk she braced herself. "Holding off thugs at gunpoint, patching up bullet holes, and cooking a gourmet meal. You're a thugs dream girl."

"Very funny, but this is hardly a gourmet meal. Just threw some ingredients together and voila."

"Closest thing I know to gourmet."

"My grandmother would have a fit if she saw me using jarred garlic, parmesan cheese out of a container, and cherry tomatoes. Now she was a first class cook. Everything from scratch, all fresh vegetables and produce."

"She teach you how to cook?"

She drew in a deep breath. Her grandmother had been one in a million. No matter what craziness went on in her family's life, she thought food could fix all. And in a way she was right. Just the smell of the onions and garlic brought Sheena back to her grandmother's tiny apartment in Brooklyn. The woman had been her rock, her female role model, her confidant and her best friend. Nothing she told her ever shocked her, and she always imparted sage advice. Solid and strong and the total opposite of her flighty mother whose only interest was the next designer bag, the next collagen treatment or the next bump of coke.

She'd often thanked whatever power reigned supreme that she had such a wonderful woman in her life, even though their time together was way too short.

"Hey." She looked up from the skillet into Cobra's beautiful face. He could easily read for a screen test for Hollywood's next mob picture. Robert DeNiro move over.

"Where'd you go, just then?"

"Just thinking about my grandmother." Nothing wrong with telling him that. Everybody had a grandmother, right. Admitting it didn't give away her dark secrets.

"You miss her?"

"She died two years ago, but yes I miss her."

"That sucks. You were close."

She felt the burning in the backs of her eyes. Tears she hadn't been able to shed at her funeral. Tears she had to hold in because of the circumstances, and the prying eyes of news vans and media cameras.

"I never knew my grandparents, barely had parents," Cobra said.

"Tough when parents let their kids down. After all, they didn't ask to be born." She looked up at him. "Do you have brothers or sisters?"

"Ahhh—No."

She stared at him for a few extra seconds. His halting way of answering threw her. It was a simple question. Either you had siblings or you didn't.

"I have a brother," she said. "But he's kind of useless."

That was an understatement. Once Angelo realized he'd never be able to measure up to her father's daunting reputation, he taken the cowards way out and drowned himself in booze, drugs and women. Not necessarily in that order, but he'd certainly never been any support or help after her life fell apart. She hadn't heard from him in over a year and sometimes wondered if his drastic lifestyle had finally caught up with him. Him and her mother were exactly the same. Selfish and self-centered.

"A brother, huh?"

She drew in another deep breath. "He's not in my life."

He leaned over the counter and grabbed her wrist. Sauce dripped into the pan as he pulled her to him. "You look cute as fuck stirring that sauce." He licked the sauce off the spoon, then pulled her in for a kiss. "It's kinda cool, you cooking for me."

"If I remember correctly you had a very beautiful woman in your kitchen not four days ago cooking you breakfast."

"That doesn't count. It was Patrice."

"A very hot woman. Why wouldn't she count."

"Because Patrice always has an agenda." He released her wrist and stared. "Do you have an agenda?"

CHAPTER ELEVEN

T he alarm on her phone buzzed telling her the pasta was ready. Saved by the mythical bell. She shut off the flame, drained the pasta into a colander, then ran cold water over it. She ladled the rigatoni into the bubbling sauce. "This is what's called marrying the sauce to the pasta."

She swirled the rigatoni around the pot until they were coated, fully aware of his eyes on her, and that she hadn't answered his question.

She plated the food, sprinkled cheese on top and handed them to him.

"How come it's two o'clock in the morning and you're as wide awake as me?" He placed the plates on the table, then stepped to the huge bar against the opposite wall. He opened a refrigerator behind the bar and pulled out a bottle of wine.

"Always alert."

"How do you manage to answer me without really answering me?" He uncorked the bottle one handed like those waiters in a fancy restaurant, and returned to the table with the wine and two glasses.

"It's a skill." She examined the label. "Opus One, nice wine." A scam involving an art dealer and a wine connoisseur made her an expert on fine wines. "One of my favorites." She'd noticed his extensive wine collection earlier. "You have quite a few expensive wines."

He shrugged, and the hard edges of his sculpted face relaxed a bit. "It's kinda a hobby."

"You really are an enigma."

"A what?"

"A riddle, a puzzle, something that doesn't connect. A tatted, hard-edged biker who knows fine wines."

He poured the wine and lifted his glass. "Here's to a scam artist who can cook a gourmet meal and an outlaw biker who knows good wine."

She sipped at it and looked across the table. "Who are you?"

"Funny, I was gonna ask you the exact same question," he countered.

The steam from the sauce mixed with their silence.

"Why don't we just enjoy." He held up his glass. "Probably should've aerated this first, but didn't want the food to get cold."

She contained her smile and forked up some rigatoni. "My grandmother would be proud." Sheena raised her glass again. "Two mysterious strangers who like to eat a big meal after midnight."

He pointed to his dish. "This is fuckin' fantastic," he said around another mouthful of sauce and pasta.

THEIR EYES MET across the table. And no it wasn't a candlelit table or any of that romantic bullshit. Just two mismatched people enjoying delicious pasta and wine.

Cobra knew good wines, 'cause along with the shots and beers he sucked up at the clubhouse, he liked wine. After doing some research he found out he liked learning about wine. The other Serpents didn't know about his hobby. Not because of his rep, but they just wouldn't get it so why bother.

His phone buzzed with a message.

Python: *I'm on my way up.*

"Shit." Cobra pushed away from the table seconds before a loud banging echoed through the room.

When he opened the door, Python bounded in. Contained energy radiating around him, then stopped short at the dining table set for two. Python arched an eyebrow at Sheena then stepped back. "Celebrating?"

The one-word question cut through the room. Python's distrust slicing into the silence. All three exchanged a look, then Sheena stood. "I'm sure you want some privacy."

Sheena retreated to the bedroom, and an uncomfortable, unexplainable guilt slithered through him.

The minute the bedroom door closed Python was on him. "What the fuck?" he bellowed.

Cobra peered over his shoulder. "Lower your damn voice."

"I don't give a shit if she hears me. You've been acting wonky since you laid eyes on her and it ain't safe."

"Not your business."

"You should've checked in and you fuckin' know it." He jerked his hand toward the table. "What the hell is this? A romantic dinner for two."

"You don't know what you're talking about."

"I figured you'd bone her, but you're usually hit it and quit it. Or did her hot snatch make you forget your responsibilities?"

Python's words ground through him.

"You better dial it down," Cobra warned.

Python threw his hands up. "And you better watch your ass 'cause this is dangerous business and that pussy is making you stupid."

"The fuck?" Cobra whipped his hand against the wine glass, and it smashed to the floor. "Did you forget I'm president of this club?"

"No, did you? You're having a nice little dinner while the rest of us are sweating our balls off?" Python slammed his hand on the table and dishes rattled. "You should've been at the Gold Mine, you should've been there representing us, but instead you were getting your dick wet."

They stared each other down. Both seething, both ready to toss in. Python had an inch and probably twenty pounds on him, but right now it didn't matter. "I'm giving you a pass because you're more than a brother, you're like my blood, but I swear to fuck you disrespect me one more time and this shit is gonna end bad."

A long, fucked up, stressed out minute passed. Eyeball to eyeball, outlaw to outlaw.

"Shit, man." Python threw his arms up. "I ain't touching you and I ain't calling you out. I just want you to stop thinking with your dick."

Cobra hated that Python was right. Hated that all he'd thought about was getting Sheena to safety. Hated that he'd let the club down, but most of all hated the feelings that coursed through him. Feelings he didn't think existed in his dysfunctional heart.

Cobra scrubbed his hand over his stubbled jaw, willing

away any introspection. Frantic to get back on track. "What's the damages?"

"Nothing to us. The DR's shot their way outta there like a scene outta Goodfella's. Metro ended up grabbing two of their prospects. Demon laughed it off. He don't give a shit about his patched brothers, much less his prospects."

"What about that guy Seth?" He'd wait to see if Sheena asked about her ex.

"He got a little busted up, but word is Metro went after the Rats. Left the dealers and even the players alone." Python pulled on the stud in his ear. "The whole thing don't make sense."

"And the money?"

"Took care of that shit first. All split up and safe at the Gold Mine. When you didn't show up I got worried. Thought Metro caught your ass. Didn't wanna say any of this shit over the phone, so I dragged myself here."

"Appreciate it, brother." They stared at each other. Python waiting for an explanation that never came.

"You're missing one hell of a party."

Cobra slapped him on the back. "I'll catch up with you tomorrow."

"I'm leaving, don't worry." Python headed for the door, then stopped and pointed toward the bedroom. "Don't get it twisted. Pussy is pussy, but the club is your life, and the two don't mix."

Cobra and Python did their usual fist bump. The door slammed and Cobra blew out a long-held breath. Python's words hit a nerve. Mainly because the annoying fucker was right. He should've been at the clubhouse after the job and he should've taken care of business. He was the goddamn president of the Serpents. Strongest club in Southern Nevada, only club in Vegas. Yet he'd let his responsibilities slide. For a woman.

It didn't make sense. Sheena openly had secrets and he knew there was plenty she was keeping from him about herself, yet in other ways her honesty blew him away. The way she looked at him during sex. Eyes wide open, eagerly waiting and wanting everything he gave her.

No screaming like a porn star trying to show off like the girls at the Gold Mine. Or like Patrice who acted aloof and detached like she was doing him a favor. Sheena's pure, honest eagerness tripped off something deep inside him. Then the tender, gentle way she patched him up. No agenda, just wanting to help him. She stirred up emotions he didn't even know existed.

His mind got so deep in thought that he missed the warning signs. The sweat pricking his forearms and the short choppy breaths startled him, then the familiar dread swept threw him. A hurricane twisting his guts and squeezing his heart. He couldn't control it and the more he tried the worse it would get.

He stumbled over to the chair by the window and crouched into the soft cushions. His gaze wandered to the lights of the Strip. Diversion, distraction, anything to make this shit stop.

OF COURSE, Sheena cracked the bedroom door and listened. Python's angry words were loud and clear, while Cobra's responses were low and dangerous. She'd heard enough to know that Python blamed her for Cobra's disappearance. Although she was happy to hear that Seth seemed to be unharmed.

Typical male, blaming the woman, but she certainly

hadn't held Cobra hostage. Granted the last time she had sex it was thirty degrees cooler, but she definitely knew when a man was into her. She doubted Cobra went without sex, yet his urgency and hunger blew her away.

Then he trusted her to take care of his wound. Almost needy, like no one had ever taken care of him before, but letting her cook in his kitchen blew her away. Where she came from cooking for someone went deeper than sex. Sharing a cooked meal bonded two people. Even if that meal was thrown together with leftovers and less than perfect ingredients, it was a sign of caring.

That revelation jarred her. She cared about Cobra. What he did, where he went, how he felt. And not in a possessive, controlling way, but in an honest, real way. The realization made her brace her hand against the wall, because caring about someone always ended badly. In her screwed-up life it usually ended in bloodshed.

The slamming of the apartment door jolted Sheena out of her brutal reality. She stepped away from the bedroom door and fussed with the bedsheets trying to act like she wasn't snooping by the door like—Like she was.

She straightened the bed and after a few more minutes she opened the door and peaked out. Cobra wouldn't have left in his sweatpants, shirtless and shoeless so he had to be here somewhere. She entered the kitchen. Empty. Then rounded the island and stopped dead. Her eyes shot to Cobra. Crouched over in one of the living room chairs. Holding his midsection, and gently rocking back and forth. So many thoughts passed through her brain. Had Python attacked Cobra, and his wound opened up?

She slowly entered the room, and stepped around the broken glass, but with his head hanging down he didn't see her. Her chest contracted at his obvious pain. When she touched his shoulder he startled, like he forgot she was in the penthouse. He raised his eyes to hers and his confusion frightened her. Had she missed something? What could cause this terrified, feral expression?

"Cobra?" She kneeled down next to the chair.

"Go in the bedroom." He leaned away from her his voice a harsh rasp.

"What's the matter. Are you in pain?" She tried unsuccessfully to keep her voice neutral.

"Just go away."

"I'm not leaving you. Now, tell me what's wrong."

As he drew in two deep breaths she examined him. His tanned skin was clammy and sallow, his eyes glassy and his breathing erratic. Did he have a heart condition or—She'd seen this exact reaction from her brother.

"Are you on something?"

"Fuck, no," he bellowed.

She jumped at his harsh response and he reached out to her.

"Tell me what's going on with you," she demanded. "Do you need a doctor?"

"No."

"Please let me help you," she pleaded, hoping a softer approach would reach him.

He turned to her and she stroked her hand over his massive, sweat covered shoulders. "It's just something I get once in a while. Nothing to worry about." He attempted a smile, but she wasn't buying it.

"Have you seen a doctor about this, because you look like shit."

He huffed out a breath. "Your honesty is gonna fuckin' kill me." He shifted in the chair, trying to smile, trying to pull it together. The effort saddened her.

"You don't have to be a tough guy with me. You can just be you, not the president of the Serpents, not the hard ass biker. Just you."

He grabbed up her hand and brought it to his lips. The gentle gesture moved her. He lowered her hand, but held tight to it.

He drew in a deep breath. "I get anxiety attacks, panic attacks, whatever the fuck you wanna call them."

She felt her mouth drop open, then quickly clamped her jaw shut. She didn't want to appear like she was judging him.

"I know, the six-foot-three badass biker gets panic attacks."

She covered her other hand over his. "No, don't do that. Your size or who you are has nothing to do with this."

"C'mon, that's was your first reaction, right?"

"No—Maybe, but only for a second. After that I just wanted to help you."

His eyes held so much anguish she looked away, then stared at their hands clasped together.

"You can't help me, but I like that you care . . . that you—"

"I don't know what this is that we have." She squeezed his hand tighter. "But you don't ever have to pretend with me. You don't ever have to be someone you're not."

He nodded and even that seemed to exhaust him.

"And don't worry, this is just between us." She pulled at his hand. "Let's get you into bed so you can rest and I'm going to clean up that kitchen."

"Nah, I got a cleaning service that comes in."

"My grandmother would roll over in her grave if she thought I left a dirty kitchen overnight." She smiled hoping to relieve some of the tension.

"We can't have that." He let her lead him into the bedroom.

He eased himself onto the edge of the bed and looked up at her. Those crystal blue eyes a little clearer. "Thank you."

CHAPTER TWELVE

Cobra reached out twice in the middle of the night. The first time was for reassurance. To feel the warmth of another body. To feel Sheena's body. Next to him, tucked into him. The only time in his life he reached for a woman for more than sex. Shit, if that wasn't a sad fuckin' commentary on his life. Thirty-three years on this damn earth and he'd never found comfort—Until now.

She snuggled into him like she knew exactly where he needed her. She wrapped her arm around his waist and settled her head on his chest, wordlessly telling him that she was there for him. Her hands never wandered below his waist, instinctively knowing that wasn't what he needed right now. His eyes closed and he drifted off again.

The second time he reached out to her that night was pure lust and need mixed in with a softer emotion he couldn't identify. And again, she responded exactly right. He gathered her in his arms and kissed her. Burying his face in her hair, then working his way to her neck. He laved the sensitive skin he'd marked earlier, then cupped her magnificent breasts. Way too tempting to be overlooked. He sucked each nipple and when she hissed in a breath, he smiled. When he got his fill he flicked his tongue over her abs, loving the soft skin against his mouth.

She pushed at him to go lower and he raised his head, smirk in place. "You tryin' to tell me something?"

"Don't tease." Her breathy whisper jacked up his pulse.

He smoothed his palms over her thighs, spreading them wide, loving the way the dim light shadowed her skin. He devoured her; not able to go slow, not able to pace himself and when she cried out he grinned against the sensitive folds. Happy to bring her there, happy to give her pleasure.

Not giving her a chance to recover he leaned over and grabbed a condom out of the nightstand drawer. Then he crawled up her body, the scent of her sex amping him up, heating his blood.

"I need you." Again, that fuckin' raspy whisper. This woman tore him apart from the inside out.

"You got me, baby." He cupped her face in his hands. "Never felt nothing special. Never wanted to." He nipped at her lips. "After tonight, you're mine. No more bullshit, no more secrets. You're with me." Her body stilled, but he continued to stare into her dark, expressive eyes. "You get it?"

She pulled him to her. His body covering her, owning her. He slid in effortlessly, like her body was made just for him. He stroked her slow and steady, filling her up, giving her way more than his cock. He'd never felt so complete, so satisfied. So real.

She'd seen him at his worst before, and yet she didn't run, she stayed. The honest way she cared for him, and relieved him of the detached isolation of suffering silently freed him. Made him believe that maybe he could find peace in his messed-up life.

He shifted and drove deeper, bracing his palms on either side of her head. Lowering himself to grab her lips with his, shove his tongue deep and claim her inside and out.

Her back stiffened and he knew she was close. "Let it go, baby. Give it all to me."

She panted and groaned, but it wasn't enough for him. "Louder, let me hear it."

When she yelled out his name followed by a string of mumbled curses he couldn't hold in. Hearing his name shouted from her lips drove him over the edge. He came hard and long, never wanting this unrelenting freedom to end. Wanting to lose himself in her body on this night forever. No Serpents, no Desert Rats, no Vinnie, not even his constant worry over Danny could screw with this high.

He rolled to her side and she wordlessly snuggled into him. Again, knowing what he needed. Silence to think his thoughts and figure out how he would bring this exceptional woman into his life.

MORNING CAME SLOWLY TO SHEENA. She stretched, reveling in the slight ache between her legs and feeling very much like a satisfied cat on a sunny day. She pushed her unruly hair out of her face and unlike the last time she woke up in Cobra's bed, she knew exactly where she was and exactly what they had done last night.

Yes, she remembered every glorious detail. His sensuous lips drawing out all her emotions, his outstanding body bringing her to the edge and holding her tight as they both fell into the abyss.

She rolled over, reached out and paused. Unfortunately, like the last time she didn't get the pleasure of waking up with him still in bed. She flopped over, and stared at the ceiling. As long as she didn't wake up to another woman in his kitchen all was good.

She listened closely to the silence, then rolled off the bed. Thankfully, unlike the last time, her head was clear. She barely finished her one glass of wine last night before Python interrupted them. She'd been annoyed at the time, but for some reason everything that came after made them closer.

"After tonight you're mine. No more secrets, no more bullshit. You're with me."

His words rang in her head, and now in the bright light of day she paused. Had he meant what he said, or—She doubted Cobra ever said anything he didn't mean. The realization of his words had her heart doing a big happy dance in her chest. Her unstable relationship with both her father and brother left her wary and cautious around men. Always. So, could it possibly be that a man she cared about cared about her too?

She threw on the same t-shirt he'd given her last night and ventured out into the penthouse. No stunning woman cooking breakfast in the kitchen thank God, no one in the whole apartment. She checked her phone. No text, no phone call, no old school scribbled message on a scrap of paper. It shook her confidence a bit, but then she chastised herself. He was a rough biker, living on his time, not used to answering to anyone.

They'd both have some adjustments to make this work. The first for her would be coming clean about her real identity and her family in New Jersey. The thought of unloading this burden thrilled her. She'd been carrying this baggage for way too long, and if Cobra could be so honest with her last night about his panic attacks then she owed him the same honesty.

She swiped at her phone.

Sheena: Leaving your apartment. Call me when you get a chance.

She hit a few heart emojis then quickly erased, them cautioning herself to take it slow.

THE BRIGHT, late morning Vegas sun shone against Cobra's face. He'd purposely gotten up early to visit Danny, leaving Sheena peacefully sleeping. He twisted the throttle and revved his engine long and loud, but picturing Danny's smile only made his heart hurt worse.

He hated that there was still a part of his life he had to share with Sheena. A part he wasn't proud of, a guilt even she couldn't dull, but like he said last night, no bullshit.

Next stop was New York Bagels, probably not the quality she was used to back East, but maybe she'd reward him for trying. That put a smile on his face. Seemed thinking about Sheena always put a smile on his face. It didn't matter if she was sassing him or wrapping her beautiful thighs around his waist, she had him grinning like a kid.

He jostled two bags in the elevator to his penthouse. One filled with an assortment of bagels and the other with an assortment of flavored cream cheese, lox and all the fixings the guy suggested that apparently went with the bagels. His morning meal usually consisted of large amounts of coffee, and a protein drink. Except when Patrice breezed in. He swore she only made pancakes and high carb shit just to piss him off. And yeah, what he held in his arms was carb overload, but somehow doing it for Sheena put a new spin on his morning routine.

His phone buzzed in his pocket but he couldn't fish it out. Then it hit him. He never texted Sheena. What if she woke up, saw him gone and left? Shit, he had a lot to learn if he wanted this to work.

When the elevator door whooshed open Sheena stood in the hallway fully dressed in her clothes from last night. He crammed both bags into his left arm and grabbed her around the waist. "Where you goin'?"

She wiggled out of his hold. "I'm leaving. When I woke up you were gone and you didn't—"

"Yeah, yeah, I know. I didn't text you. My bad, but you gotta give me a pass. This shit is new to me."

"What exactly do you mean by *this shit*?" She slammed her hands on her hips.

He grinned, then slipped his free arm through hers and led her to his door. She acted like she was resisting, but he caught the glimmer in her eyes. She was enjoying this as much as him.

"You think just because you're bigger than me you can just—"

He turned her to him, and lowered his lips to hers. A second later, their tongues were teasing each other. "You got anything else to say?"

She bit her lower lip and he knew she tasted him.

He nudged her into the apartment, and placed the bags on the kitchen counter.

"What's all this?" She peeked into one of the bags. "Bagels?"

"Since you cooked for me last night, I figured I'd bring you breakfast. You mentioned that New Jersey was known for their bagels. Probably won't be as good but—"

She leaned up and gave him another head spinning kiss, and fuck if his cock didn't stand up at attention. He knew what that selfish sucker wanted, but he had other ideas.

"You got any plans for today?" Normally he told people

what to do, so asking was new to him. So was the fluttery sensation in his gut as he waited for her answer. Not a fan.

"No. My next shift at the Pirate's Cove is tomorrow night."

"And you won't be dealing for Vinnie anymore."

"No, I guess not."

VINNIE POPPED into Sheena's head a few times this morning. From what she overheard last night between Cobra and Python, the games were all raided. She assumed Vinnie would lay low for a while especially since Metro showed up, but two things still gnawed at her. What was Cobra and Vinnie's connection? And could she trust Cobra with the truth about her past?

His icy blue eyes peered through her and her brain spun with all the ways she could tell him her true idenity. Just put it out there and get it over with.

"You ever been to the Grand Canyon?"

She'd been so caught up in her mental drama she thought she misunderstood him.

"The Grand Canyon?"

"They got a thing called the Skywalk where you walk out over the canyon. Fuckin' amazing."

CHAPTER THIRTEEN

"You forgot to mention that the floor was glass and we're thousands of feet in the air." Sheena hated heights. Her pulse ramped up, and her palms were clammy with sweat. Good times.

"C'mon, babe, it's safe. The sign said you could land a 747 on it." He jumped up and down a few times, and she shivered.

"Stop." She flailed her arms around. "The sign also said we're 4000 feet in the air."

People around them giggled, and she inched her way out of the main building so other people could pass her.

"You come out here and I'll buy you an ice cream." Cobra wheedled extending his hand.

"I'm not a child."

Cobra closed the distance between them, and leaned into her ear. "You do this and I'll make you come so hard tonight, that you won't be able to walk for a week."

Her cheeks heated. "You should've led with that." She baby stepped out over the glass floor, hugging the center of the bridge.

Cobra leaned against the outer railing overlooking the canyon. "C'mere so we can take a selfie. The view is incredible."

She scrunched up her face and he laughed. Some other people invested in their little drama chimed in. "Go on." An older, grandmotherly type stepped up. "I'll take your picture."

Cobra handed her his phone and the woman smiled. "Go on, honey. You don't want to keep this luscious man waiting."

Everybody around them cheered, and egged her on until she had no choice. She let go of the inside railing and tiptoed to the other side, afraid that any false move would crack the glass and they would all plummet to their deaths. That thought froze her in place until Cobra reached out and pulled her the rest of the way.

"You know, you spend a lot of time pulling me around?"

He lifted her at her waist and kissed her full on the mouth. Their audience cheered, as the older woman snapped shot after shot.

Sheena pretended to struggle, then gave up and they both mugged for the camera.

"You two are very sweet." The woman handed Cobra his phone, a huge smile plastered onto her kind face. "Ahhh, to be in love again."

Sheena laughed, and thanked the woman, pretending not to hear the word 'love.'

"I told you we looked good together." Cobra pulled her to his side as they made their way around the horseshoe shaped bridge. At the furthest point her legs wobbled, and Cobra held her tighter. Again, knowing what she needed when she needed it.

They finally returned to the main building and she let out a sigh of relief, which Cobra laughed at.

"I can't believe you. Double dealing high stakes poker,

keeping it together during a gunfight, and patching up my bullet wound, but you're afraid of heights." Cobra kissed the top of her head, and the simple gesture was more intimate than anything they'd gotten up to the night before.

She'd been wrong so many other times with men, misread their signals. Her head and common sense told her to calm down, and not jump to conclusions, but her heart—

They walked through the gift shop and he stopped. "I think we need to get you a t-shirt that says, "I did the Skywalk."

She pulled a few full-sized t-shirts off the rack and he scrunched up his lips. "Nah, you need something to show off that beautiful figure." He moved to a display with skimpy tank tops. "This is what I'm talking about."

"You sure?" Tank tops and her had a hate/hate relationship. If they weren't exposing too much of her full bosom, they were riding up on her rounded hips.

He came up behind her, firmly planting his hands on her hips, then lowered his head to her ear. "Positive."

His warm breath against her ear and the sneaky grin that went with it had her toes curling in her low leather boots.

After picking out a color in her size, she was the proud owner of a t-shirt with a picture of the Grand Canyon Skywalk and the words, "I did it."

As they stood in line in the crowded gift shop, Sheena noticed the women who openly admired Cobra. Some less discreet than others. Sheena's first reaction centered around calling some of them out, but she reconsidered. In their defense, it was difficult not to notice a six-foot-three guy with muscles covered in intricate tats draped in a black t-shirt and faded jeans that hit all the right places.

But that wasn't all. Cobra's scruff around his jawline, multiple silver rings, leather bands around his left wrist and the snake stud winding around his earlobe said edgy biker, while his straight nose and square sculpted jaw said Hollywood leading man. He carried himself in an easy way, graceful for a man of his size, with just the right amount of swagger. Sheena guessed some of them did a double take thinking he was someone from their latest Netflix binge.

Outside, they walked along a path that rimmed the west side of the canyon. The colors from different angles, and the reflection of the sun against the rock amazed her. She'd spent five years in Las Vegas, but rarely left the city. Afraid that venturing too far away from her home base would bring trouble. Similar to the sensation of walking on that glass bridge. If she kept her life tight and capsulized she would be safe.

The beauty of this untouched canyon evoked a fearlessness in her. Putting her in touch with something greater than her secrets. She'd never seen anything so magnificent. They stopped a few times to take more selfies, and as the sun lowered he suggested they leave.

She had a hard time drawing her eyes away from the majestic natural wonder. Oh, and the Grand Canyon too. Sometimes she just couldn't turn off the sass in her mind. Sometimes she had to literally bite the inside of her cheek to prevent her thoughts from spilling out of her mouth.

They made their way to the parking lot, and his Harley. Although she was looking forward to the ride back, she hated to see the day end. He stored the bag with her t-shirt, sat sideways on the seat and pulled her between his legs.

He brushed her wild curls away from her face and gazed down at her. His eyes soft and warm. "I had fun today."

"Me too." She wanted to say so much more. Like, It's the best time I've had in—ever.

"Next time we'll go up to Mount Charleston. I got a cabin up there. Really beautiful."

Next time? She mashed her lips together. Him talking about taking her to his cabin meant seeing him again, which meant—Her throat tightened and for some strange reason her eyes burned with tears.

"You all right?"

Shit, nothing got past this man.

"I'm fine," she said much too quickly. Great. Master scam artist, card mechanic, and she couldn't control her voice to say two words without giving herself away.

Her face heated under his scrutiny. Another thing that seldom happened. Her olive complexion rarely flamed, yet here she was blushing like a—virgin, or a schoolgirl. You name it, because she certainly couldn't.

His arms circled around her waist, pulling her tighter to him.

She looked over her shoulder. "We're not alone, you know?"

"Do I look like a man who gives a shit what others think?"

She shrugged. "Guess not." Truth. She didn't care either, but her usual banter flew out of her mind along with any common sense, leaving her with annoying, generic small talk.

He took her mouth in a gentle kiss that soon became heated. So heated that her traitorous hips ground into him, and oh yeah, it felt so good. The low growl from his throat told her he liked it too. His hands dropped to her ass, cupping her with his palms, molding her to his body. Thank God for the stable Harley holding them up or she'd be tempted to embarrass herself and drag him down into the dirt parking lot. In front of the tour buses, vans full of families, and elderly onlookers.

He broke away from her lips, his smile a devilish grin.

"Remember we got a two-hour drive to Vegas, and I can't handle the bike with a hard-on."

"Ahhh, poor baby."

"You're not teasing me, right?" He squeezed her ass. "Cause you know what happens when you tease me."

"I can take it."

"You sure can." He dug his hand into her hair holding her head in his palm. "I like this. I like us."

"I like this too, but there's no us." She had to test him. Sure, last night he'd said some things, but everyone knew sex talk was different than bright daylight talk. "Face it, we barely know each other."

Her words surprised her, like her thoughts magically fell out of her mouth. Usually she had more control, usually she kept her feelings to herself.

"I know I like you in my bed. I think I told you that last night."

So he did remember. Score one for the biker.

His hooded gaze fell to her lips. "I know I like everything your mouth does. Whether it's sucking my dick or throwing sass in my face. You light me up, babe."

"I agree the sex was good but—"

"Good? Are you fuckin' kidding me? Our bodies are made for each other."

A replay of the last twenty-four hours ignited a flame that blazed in her middle. She tried to step away and put some distance between them.

"Sheena?" His voice low, a warning tone.

"We've spent one day together, but that doesn't mean we know each other."

"I know you like to cook, I know you make a damn good nurse, and I know you're afraid of heights." He laughed. "Just sayin' I think that's more than I've ever known about a woman before."

No, she refused to be fooled into thinking he cared about her.

"And yeah, I know that sounds kinda shitty, but I want you to know that whatever we got is real."

How she wanted to act like a silly teenager and hang on his every word, but she knew better. Didn't she?

"Let's put this away for now. Get on my bike." He handed her the helmet. "And head to Vegas."

"Fine. I can do that." She secured the helmet on her head.

His hands covered hers as she fiddled with the straps. "But this isn't done."

His eyes pierced through the face guard of the helmet and she swallowed hard. Then he put his own helmet on and threw his leg over the wide Harley seat.

Maybe this could work, maybe they did have a chance, or maybe his hotness in bed numbed her brain and made her stupid. Made her believe in a dream as she headed for a nightmare.

THE MINUTE they crossed the Nevada border Cobra pulled to the shoulder, unlocked his saddlebag, and threw on his cut. Sheena followed his movements.

"Didn't wanna stir up shit in Colorado," he offered. "Only wear my colors in my home state, unless we're at a rally."

She furrowed her brow, remembering some of the club rules Daisy filled her in on when she'd gotten with Joker. It always struck her as odd. For a group of bikers whose motto centered around freedom, they had lots of rules. Stringent rules, that if broken could have disastrous results.

The importance of his life in the club and the men he called brothers wouldn't change, and she would never ask him to change, but the lifestyle was radical. Another variable to consider if she pursued whatever she and Cobra had, or whatever he thought they had together.

"Only another forty-five minutes. You wanna stretch your legs a bit?"

"No, I'm good." In truth, her spine was stiff and her legs were cramped, but she feared another talk about the next steps of whatever this was between them.

Her brief experience on a motorcycle consisted of rides that didn't last longer than twenty minutes. Similar to her experiences with men. And there it was again, that sass. Could be the reason for her short-term relationships, but Cobra seemed to like it, or so he said.

He kicked the huge machine to life and Sheena willed herself to relax against his broad, firm back. She let the speed, dry desert air and the smell of leather clear her mind, as the Harley ate up the nearly deserted span of highway to Vegas. Such an unusual land. Barren, rocky sand with scrubby bushes and low cactus, then in the distance the majestic mountain range which now, in the setting sun, gave off a rainbow of colors and contrasts. A sight this Jersey girl would always appreciate.

CHAPTER FOURTEEN

Forty-five minutes later Cobra pulled into the garage of his building, then backed into his designated spot. He busied himself locking down the bike and storing the helmets, then handed her the bag with her t-shirt.

She stayed silent. The two-hour ride had given her more than enough time to think and evaluate every word Cobra said in that parking lot. Stark truths flowed over her like the dry desert air. If a hardened biker could open up and be honest than he deserved the same from her. Not just her feelings for him, but everything about her. She'd hidden behind lies long enough and if she was going to do this than Cobra deserved the truth.

They stared at each other over the bike. His phone buzzed in his pocket and he fished it out, then swiped at the screen. She'd been so locked in her own thoughts that she missed his silence. Maybe the two-hour ride had him regretting his words, and now he was looking for a way to take them back.

No, damn it. Get rid of all that negative energy. He meant what he said, and you are worth it.

He put the phone to his ear and she assumed he was listening to missed messages after the two-hour trip.

He listened for a few more minutes. Gave a few grunts and then. "I gotta go." His face grim.

"Okay." And what was she to do? Wait in the garage? Leave? Go up to his apartment and wait for him? Her confidence plummeted along with the large rock forming in her stomach.

"I gotta get over to the Gold Mine. You want me to call you an Uber?"

Questions answered. He was sending her off. Yup, now everything was right with the world.

She whipped out her phone. It gave her something to hold to camouflage the trembling of her hands. "No, I got it."

"I'll probably be a while."

"Sure, no problem." How many times had she said those words? How many times had she acted cool and composed, like the brush off didn't hurt? She knew how this would go. The ghosting of her calls and messages until she couldn't deny the truth.

She gripped the plastic shopping bag in her fist. At least this time she had a souvenir of another disastrous fail.

She stepped away from the bike and he grabbed her forearm. She stared at his hand but he didn't remove it.

"You all right?"

Sure, just fine. I'm used to being run over by a bus. Doesn't even hurt anymore. Or in this case, a Harley driven by a heartbreakingly beautiful man that would never be hers.

The dead heat of the garage surrounded her, sucking out every ounce of emotion. She raised the plastic bag in her sweaty hand. "Thanks."

She scanned the cement structure, finding the exit sign

only a few feet away. He leaned over the seat of the Harley, but she already stepped away.

"I'll call you."

Right. Of course, he wouldn't. She wanted to run, but didn't want to give him the satisfaction, so she walked very quickly to the big, red exit sign. For some absurd reason the Monopoly game came to mind. Do not pass go, do not collect $200, do not admit that your heart is breaking.

COBRA DREW IN THE DRY, dense air. He'd definitely fucked that up. Saying all that shit to her before, he fuckin' spooked her. Granted, he was new to this relationship shit, but he really blew it.

He'd always kept things simple. Sex, a couple of beers at the clubhouse, fine. Conversation, long term shit, and talking about feelings, not so much. What the hell was he thinking? He didn't know how to do this shit, and the way she just looked at him. He should've at least offered her a ride home.

Fuck! She couldn't get away fast enough. She bolted out of here like the damn place was on fire. What the hell did he expect? A classy girl like her would never want to share his life. He was an outlaw biker for crissake, and she was trying get her life straight. She sure didn't want to get knee deep in his shit. Dumping his ass was a no brainer.

He scanned over the missed calls and text messages from Python—Where the fuck are you? What the fuck are you doing? And answer your fuckin' phone, we gotta set up a meet. He thumbed the screen and sent all the officers a message to meet him at the Gold Mine.

He hopped on his bike and revved the engine, then he sped down the narrow aisles of the garage taking each turn faster than the last. Anything to get rid of this pissed off, amped up rock in his gut. In the bad old days he would've snorted a few lines, but experience told him that never worked. Only made the shit that surged through him worse.

By the time he got to the Gold Mine he'd sorted a few things out. Get his club business done, then he'd call her. Make things right. He hoped.

The Gold Mine at seven at night was relatively quiet. A few guys at the bar, a few more playing pool, and some club girls hanging out by the TV's.

Cobra headed to the back room. Tonight's meeting was just for officers. Python, his Sargent at Arms, Rattler, their Treasurer and Boa, their Road Captain. The club still lacked a VP, but Cobra wasn't done trying to sway Joker into the job.

Cobra sat at the head of the table and the other three men settled around him.

"Missed you, brother." Rattler's less than discreet way of saying 'Where the fuck you been?'

"I'm here now." Cobra leveled him with a glare.

Rattler patted his pockets for his smokes. Message received.

"The DR's are back in Laughlin." Boa shifted his bulk in the wooden chair. "I had some of the prospects follow their asses all the way to the border. Just to make sure they got gone."

"Don't need any more crazy than necessary."

Silence surrounded them.

"All right, I'll say it." Python lit up a joint. "What the hell was Metro doing at the warehouse on Valley View? They've known about those games for months. Why now?"

"Been thinking the same thing." Cobra pulled a cigarette out of Rattler's pack and Python lit him up. He dragged deep and blew the smoke toward the ceiling. "Especially since none of Vinnie's people got hauled in. All they got were a few Rat prospects."

"Valley View was the third place the Rats hit. Maybe somebody tipped off Vinnie and instead of taking care of it himself, he let Metro do it."

"He pays them enough." Rattler ashed his cigarette. "Might as well put them to good use."

"Nah." Boa slapped his meaty palm against the table. "Why would he call them on his own game? Don't make sense."

"It does if you have an agenda." Cobra ground out. "And Vinnie always has an agenda."

"The cops were only interested in us outlaws." Python reasoned. "If the DR's hadn't opened fire, the cops would've dragged both clubs in. It's like they knew we were gonna be there."

Python's outlook silenced them all. The idea that somebody set them up, or that they might've been the target changed everything. These four men trusted each other with their lives and even the suggestion of betrayal stung deep.

Only Python knew about his relationship with Sheena, and Cobra hoped that wasn't the road he was taking.

"I'll pay Vinnie a visit at Ecstasy." Cobra broke into their thoughts. "Lay it all out for him once and for all. No more bullshit, no more threats. He either backs the fuck down, or things get messy."

"And by messy, you mean body bags?" Rattler asked.

"I mean whatever gets the job done."

Grunts and *fuck yeahs* filled the room as they filed out. Cobra wasn't surprised when Python stayed behind.

"What's up?" Python passed him the joint and Cobra waved him away. "C'mon, you should at least sample our own product. We got the best weed in Southern Nevada."

Python held it out again, and Cobra snatched it up, sucking in deep. He let the thick smoke coat his throat and fill his lungs. "Forgot how good our shit was," he choked out around a cloud of smoke.

"So, where were you all day? I texted and called you, but—"

"Grand Canyon." One thing Cobra hated was questions.

"What the hell were you doin' at Grand fuckin' Canyon?"

"Taking a day off."

Python pulled a face, then reached for the joint.

Cobra sucked in two deep drags, finished it off, then flicked the burn out into the ashtray. A dick move for sure, but right now Python's attitude pissed him the fuck off. "Even Wall Street execs get a day off, right?" The heavy scented smoke billowed between them in the small room.

"Wall Street suits don't handle distribution of a couple hundred pounds of weed a week, or have a psycho like Vinnie breathing down their backs. You should've answered your goddamn phone."

Cobra slammed his palms against the scarred wood and leaned in. "That's the second fuckin' time in twenty-four hours you've gotten in my business."

"That's because you're forgetting about business." Python stood with him, eye to eye across the narrow table. "Big fuckin' coincidence that your girl just happens to be dealing for Vinnie the same night Metro shows up, or are you so deep in that pussy that you ain't seeing straight. That bitch is twisting you up."

Cobra's arm shot out and grabbed Python by the t-shirt.

"Hey, what the hell!" Boa barged into the room, and yanked the two apart. Cobra and Python glared at each other, then Cobra pointed at Python. "You better watch your damn self."

Python's chest rose and fell with pent up anger simmering very close to the surface.

"Good thing I came back for my smokes." Boa switched a look between them. "What the hell is goin' on?"

"Nothing." Cobra and Python grunted in unison.

"We got enough shit without you two mixing it up." Boa swiped his smokes off the table. "Try to play nice, huh." He left, shutting the door behind him.

Python pulled at the neck of his t-shirt, then stormed out of the room.

Cobra stayed behind. Fuckin' son of a bitch, getting up in his face again. Calling him out and talking shit. Who the fuck did he think he was? He braced his hands against the table and his mind spun.

Or was he talking truth? Shit, could Python be right? Was what he thought he felt for Sheena all bullshit? Was she making him believe something that wasn't true? She'd made a life out of conning people so maybe he was just another mark.

He'd admit that a woman never got to him like her. The way she looked at him, the way they were in bed. How she patched him up, cooled him out after his panic attack. Nah, nobody could play him that good.

Time to take matters into his own hands. He grabbed his phone out of his pocket and speed dialed Vinnie's number.

"You've got a lot of balls calling me." Vinnie's low rasp barely contained his venom.

"You at Ecstasy?"

"Yes."

"Stay there. We need to talk."

Cobra didn't wait for an answer. He swiped the phone and jammed it into his jeans pocket. His breathing heaved in and out, his pulse quickened.

Oh fuckin' no, not now. He had shit to do. He gripped the edge of the table and willed the debilitating sensations away. His heart slowed and his vision cleared. Yeah, he could do this.

He slammed out of the office and found Python by the bar. "I'm heading over to Ecstasy. Gonna get shit straight with Vinnie, once and for all."

"Alone?" Python's way of leaving the question open ended.

"I'm also gonna find out Sheena's connection to him, and put all this bullshit undercurrent to rest."

Python cocked his head. "Good luck with that, brother."

They stared each other down then tapped fists. Cobra saw the questions in Python's eyes, but it would take more than heated words to break their bond, and right now that was probably exactly what Vinnie wanted. Undermine them from the inside so it would be easier to take over from the outside, but not this time. Vinnie liked to pull the strings, but the Serpents were too strong to be manipulated. Time had come to man the fuck up.

CHAPTER FIFTEEN

The twenty-minute ride to Ecstasy felt like hours. He liked Sheena on the back of his bike and right now he missed her beautiful body pressed against him. She rode like a pro, moving with him on the turns, sensing his movements. Just like when they were in bed. Sheena and him were equals, looking for that next high. Pushing each other past all limits. Perfect comparison for two renegades, neither one afraid even when life sent them over a cliff.

Cobra pulled into his spot behind Ecstasy mentally preparing himself for whatever bullshit Vinnie threw his way. He'd make it clear that from now on the Serpents were on their own. No more sharing profits, no more doing things his way. The Serpents would be taking over the weed farm and putting back the old employees. And if the stupid fucker didn't get it, Cobra would point out that knocking over five of his biggest earners made their agreement was null and void.

Then he'd find Sheena and fix the bullshit way he'd handled things this afternoon. He'd explain to her that he was a dumb shit when it came to relationships, but he was willing to try. Willing to do what it took to make it work between them. As pissed as he was with Vinnie, the thought of Sheena made him smile.

The club hummed with the usual evening crowd. Guys getting off the day shift, guys taking a late dinner break and guys just plain hanging out eyeballing the woman. He nodded to the bouncers and stopped halfway to the bar.

Fuckin' unbelievable. The man never stopped playing games. Vinnie sat at the bar with Patrice hugged up tight between his legs, her arms wrapped around his neck and her trademark pout firmly in place. He guessed this was supposed to upset him, but frankly he was relieved.

He sauntered over to them, unable to contain the smirk. "You do like to live dangerously," Cobra deadpanned, eyes on Vinnie.

"Or, I just know a good thing when I see it." Vinnie ran his finger down Patrice's neck, and she giggled. Patrice didn't giggle.

"You did me a favor, man. Now I don't have to worry about letting her down gently."

Patrice's back stiffened and her eyes shone against the strobe lighting.

Cobra cocked his head. "But I gotta tell you, that snatch ain't as tight as you might think."

Patrice lunged, Vinnie held her arm and Cobra laughed long and loud. "Yup, you did me a solid."

Patrice's nose flared as she tried to contain herself. Vinnie stood, whispered something in her ear, and she flounced away.

"If this little show is over, can we get down to it." Cobra glared at Vinnie.

They settled at Vinnie's table, and Cobra pulled out his smokes.

"I don't like losing." Vinnie ground out. "Losing money, losing power, or losing people whom I thought I could trust."

Vinnie loved to talk in circles, but Cobra wasn't having it. He wanted to get this done.

"We lost trust a long fuckin' time ago." Cobra stuck the cigarette between his lips. "Hard to have trust when you're partner's trying to screw you."

Vinnie leaned in. "I know you were behind the raids last night. Getting the Rats to do the job wasn't very original."

"And smuggling underage women to run the weed farms and forcing them to do porn isn't what we signed up for." Cobra drew deep on his smoke. "That shit ain't right, plus it's got a long fuckin' jail time and I don't want me or any of my brothers to end up in the joint because you're trying to make an extra buck in the flesh trade."

Cobra leaned back in the chair willing his body to relax.

"Looks like we're at a turning point."

Cobra hit his smoke again. "Time for us to cut our loses. Agree to disagree. Go our own way."

Cobra wasn't worried. According to Python, their take from the hit on the poker games was up in the six figures, and Cobra and the Serpents knew enough about the weed business to run the farms by themselves. Plus they had all the pissed off workers Vinnie fired, just begging to get their jobs back and stick it to the cocksucker. Once upon a time, they needed Vinnie's money and connections, but that bill was paid long ago.

Vinnie mashed his lips together as he drummed his fingers against the table. Cobra never knew what kind of shit rolled around in his twisted mind, but this time he had him, this time Vinnie had no way out. So just take the deal and move on sucker.

"Life has so many twists and turns, don't you agree?"

Great. Now he was getting philosophical.

"So many things we don't understand."

Cobra smashed his cigarette butt into the ashtray. "I laid it all out for you. No more partnership, no more sharing the profits. We're done."

Vinnie cocked his head, and waited a beat. "I can understand your need for more funds. Must be very expensive to keep your brother at such a high-end facility."

Cobra's ears roared as his blood surged through his body. "What the fuck are you talking about?"

"Your brother, Danny, the one you put in the wheelchair."

Cobra leaned across the table until he was in Vinnie's face. "How did you—"

"I'm not as dumb-witted as those bikers you hang with, plus it's very valuable to know everyone's Achilles heel. Unlike you, I investigate the people I do business with." Vinnie played with his cocktail napkin. "Some terrible accidents can happen to people in wheelchairs."

Cobra's hand shot across the table and grabbed Vinnie by his starched shirt dragging him to his feet. "You better never mention my brother again," Cobra hissed through clenched teeth.

"No need to, I think you got the message." Vinnie sneered.

"You need some help, boss?" One of the bouncers flanked Cobra.

Cobra twisted Vinnie's shirt in his fist, then released him.

Vinnie smoothed his palm over his shirt and jacket, righted his chair and sat. "That's not the only secret you might be interested in hearing."

Cobra waved away the bouncer, and stood. "Go fuck yourself and your secrets."

"Even if they concern the woman you fucked last night?"

Cobra stilled, his hands gripping the edge of the table.

"Or the real reason she was dealing that game?"

A heat surrounded Cobra's neck. "Don't mess with me."

"She's good at what she does. Getting close to you, getting into your penthouse and then the big payoff. Getting you to rescue her at the Valley View warehouse." Vinnie sucked in a deep satisfying breath. "I admit things didn't end as they should've. Wasn't planning on you having so much back up."

"What the hell are you talking about? The cops showed up."

"Of course they did. I called them."

Cobra tried to school his reaction, but his body folded into the chair, mesmerized by Vinnie's revelation.

"The plan was to get you there. Which Sheena accomplished, and then a deadly shootout." Vinnie pursed his lips. "Sometimes things just don't go as planned."

"Nah, I'm not falling for this shit. She didn't even tell me she was gonna be there."

"Of course she didn't. A good con is about finesse."

"That whole heist was on the Serpents." Cobra twisted the snake ring on his middle finger. "We pulled security and then set the DR's on your places. She had nothing to do with it."

"You just don't get it do you?" Vinnie slowly let his eyes rake over him. "Next time you see that dark haired cunt ask her about her father, and the real reason she ran to Vegas and changed her name." Vinnie studied him waiting for a reaction. "And how and why she was involved in his murder."

Cobra's mind spun in all different directions. Sheena evaded and avoided every question he asked her. First using sex and then using food by cooking for him, and he let her slide. Sure, she pulled him through his panic attack but was that just another way to lure him in? Make him trust her. Gain his confidence. No, not fuckin' possible.

"I see by your silence that you're not quite sure of your new bedmate, so I guess you better ask her yourself. Only use her given name. Serena Victoria Cipriani."

She told him she changed her name. Part of Cobra wanted to call bullshit on him, but the smarter half knew the truth. Vinnie was a vindictive piece of shit who ruled people by their secrets. Played with their lives by pulling their strings until they snapped.

"I think you'll find, with her family background, that setting you up at an underground poker game was easy."

Vinnie pushed away from the table and stood. "Remember, she came to me and even though I've been looking after her since she got out here, I thought you deserved to know the truth."

Cobra watched Vinnie saunter down the back hall and then out of the club. His words ringing in his head. Trying to figure out timelines, past conversations, and that name, Cipriani. He whipped out his phone and hit Wiki, then stared in disbelief.

Angelo Cipriani—born November 26, 1965—Brooklyn, NY.

Angelo Cipriani's teenage years were molded by the men who controlled his neighborhood in Brooklyn. Looking up to their example, he rose to fame and notoriety as one of the most ruthless mob bosses in Brooklyn. Marrying his childhood sweetheart, Victoria, he moved the family to New Jersey where he continued his reign of crime. His son Angelo Jr. was born in 1988, and a daughter Serena Victoria was born in 1991.

Cobra skipped over the lists of arrests and scrolled down to *Death.*

133

It is alleged that Angelo's daughter Serena was indirectly responsible for his murder. After a short trial, and a barrage of high-priced lawyers, a mistrial was declared.

Fuck! Cobra reread the bio three more times. No wonder she was so secretive, but it didn't change the facts. Fuckin' Vinnie was right. And if he was right about her past history he was probably right about everything else. All the shit she said and did was just part of a long con. And he'd fallen for it —Hard.

What a fuckin' asshole he'd been, telling her about his cabin on Mt. Charleston. Thinking they might've had a future. Her and Vinnie must've gotten a good laugh at that one.

A weakening calm slinked through him. His body didn't even have the energy for a panic attack. His gut twisted with her deceit but what really got to him was that he believed her. All at once everything became too much. Too much worrying, too much guilt, too much—Bullshit.

He pushed himself away from the table and stood in the back of the club. Two dancers went on and off the stage before he had the strength to move. A vacant chair at the end of the long bar lured him in.

Oh yeah, he planned on getting good and drunk. Clarissa smiled at him from behind the bar then appeared with a shot glass and a bottle of tequila like she knew what he needed.

He didn't realize he'd poured the shot until the silver liquid burned his throat. The second one went down easy and he didn't even feel the third one. The numbness in his throat matched the rest of him.

"You know that was an act before." Familiar fingers skated down his spine, as a cloud of perfume surrounded him. "Vinnie playing his games."

He turned to the side, propping his head on his fist. Didn't she know he just wanted to get trashed by himself.

"The truth isn't always easy to hear." The absolute sincerity in Patrice's voice made him roar with laughter.

"Are you fuckin' kidding me, right now? You wouldn't know truth if it fucked you in the ass." That should get rid of her.

He gripped the tequila bottle, angled it toward the glass, then pushed the glass away. "Screw it, who needs a glass." He slugged it straight from the bottle, wiped his mouth with the back of his hand, then glared at Patrice. "Are you still here?"

"You can try to fight what we have, but I'm the only one still by your side."

"What we have, what we've always had is nothing more than a quick fuck. A place for me to empty my balls." That even sounded shitty to his ears.

"You could've left, but you didn't." She pressed to his side angling her tits against his bicep.

"Got nowhere else to go." He rested his head in his hands.

"I knew you wouldn't leave," she whispered in his ear. Her breath was hot against his ear, so he shifted away from her and gulped down more tequila. "We're all we've got." With the lights shadowing her face, the hard lines and fierce determination faded and almost made her seem innocent. Almost.

What right did he have to wish for something better, something good? He'd failed the only person that loved him and put him in a wheelchair. Sheena betraying him was just what he deserved.

Her fingers flirted with the waist of his jeans. "Two empty souls, two empty hearts."

Fuck, she was right.

"YOU'RE WRONG, and no I don't want another glass of wine."
Sheena waved Daisy away. "Damn liquor got me into this
mess in the first place." Sheena pushed away her empty glass
on the small table wedged between the deck chairs on Daisy's
terrace.

After their disastrous departure in the parking garage,
Sheena called Daisy in a panic and then called an Uber. Daisy
being a good friend insisted that she come to her condo, but
now Sheena was beginning to regret her decision.

"Thinking that Cobra and I could've had something real.
It only took him a two-hour ride to realize he'd made a huge
mistake." Sheena traced her finger around the rim of her wine
glass. "Thinking that he cared. What a fucking joke I am."

"You're exaggerating, as usual." Daisy flicked her hand in
a very annoying way. "And I'm not wrong. These guys like to
talk shit to each other, but when it comes down to it, they
don't say what they don't mean, and if Cobra talked about
seeing you in the future, then he meant it."

She wanted to believe Daisy more than she realized. This
wasn't just about another failed relationship or another relationship that didn't get off the ground. This was about feelings that she didn't even know existed. Or feeling anything
since her exile to Las Vegas.

"I just don't know what happened. First he was saying
what a good time he had and about seeing me again, and then,
poof—He's giving me the brush off." Sheena wiped at her
brow. "Ninety freaking degrees and it's only April." The
dark, dry, breezeless night pulled at her last nerve.

"You're being dramatic. Why would he do that?"

"Have you met me? I'm like some kind of weird repellant
when it comes to men." Sheena waved her arms around. "The

minute I get interested in one, they vanish. The military should use me on the front lines."

"Who are you and what have you done with my friend, Sheena?" Daisy refilled her glass and held it up. "The kick-ass girl I first met when I came to Vegas. The one who could pass herself off as a Greek heiress or a DEA agent."

Sheena smiled in spite of herself. "I still remember the look on Joker's face when we barged into that office with our DEA jackets and fake badges. He literally looked like he was going to piss himself."

"Right, so what's all this whining and second guessing yourself? I doubt Cobra was brushing you off. There's a lot going on with the club right now. The Serpents have been trying to break away from Vinnie even before you two hooked up and now—"

"But that's it. I thought this was more than a hook up. Believe me, I've had plenty of hook ups, but this seemed different, this seemed real."

"Just give him time. Men are like trees, they take forever to grow up."

"Reallly? That's all you've got?"

"Sorry, I read it on Instagram the other day. Thought it was funny."

"Great, my whole life is falling apart, and you're quoting weird meme's from Instagram." Sheena flopped against the cushions. "By now he's probably at Ecstasy ogling naked girls."

"He runs Ecstasy. I'm sure he's way over naked women."

"What man ever gets over naked women?"

"It's probably like working in a bakery. You get tired of looking at all the cupcakes and sweets."

"You really need to stop with these analogies. You're killing me."

"I'm just saying that I'm sure he's not there with his tongue hanging out. He's probably in his office doing paperwork."

"What man would be in his office when there's half naked women on stage with fabulous bodies?"

"A man who wants a real woman. A man that doesn't want to stare at a bunch of giraffes pumped up with silicone and collagen. A man who already found a good woman."

"Yeah, right."

"There's one way to find out." Daisy drained her wine, then jumped up.

"I know I'm not going to like whatever you're going to say next."

"Fine, sit your sorry ass here and do nothing, or come with me to Ecstasy and stake your claim. How else will he know how you feel if you don't tell him?" Daisy swayed slightly, then braced her hand on the sliding glass door.

"Well, you're in no condition to drive."

"Of course not." Daisy rummaged through her bag, then threw Sheena her keys. "But you are so—Let's go."

CHAPTER SIXTEEN

C obra's boots scuffed against the stairs to Patrice's second floor apartment. He tripped over the last step and gripped the bannister, righting himself. "Fuckin' stairs." He barked out a laugh and it echoed against the cement walls of the stairwell.

He stopped on the landing, swayed, flung his arm around Patrice's shoulders and slammed both of them into the cinder block wall. He wasn't sure who was keeping who upright.

He fisted the bottle and gulped at the tequila, then held it up to her lips. "C'mon babe, you're not gonna let me drink alone."

She took a hit, handed him back the bottle, then pushed through the door into the hallway that led to her apartment. She unlocked the door and he stumbled into her living room doing a half turn, then bracing himself against the sofa.

"I'm really fucked up." He squinted at Patrice, trying to focus. Was she smiling at him or smirking at him? So hard to tell with her, even when he was stone cold sober. Definitely too much thinking so he flopped down on the couch, sprawled his legs out, and propped the bottle on his thigh.

"I got some shit that will straighten you right out." Patrice pulled a baggie of fine white powder out of an end table drawer, then sat next to him on the couch.

She arranged the neat lines on the glass top coffee table, then held out one of the small straws to him.

"Nah, I'll stick with the booze." Him and coke had a dicey relationship and even his tequila swamped brain told him that would be a bad idea.

Patrice shrugged, leaned over and hovered up two lines like a champ. She sat up, blinked a few times then went in for the third. Impressive. No wonder she was able to stay up till the club closed at five am.

She wiped at her nose then turned to him with a bright smile. "Crazy. I feel like I haven't drank a thing."

"Right, now your brain is spun another way."

She eased the tequila out of his fist and placed it on the table. "It's been a while since you've been up here."

Cobra stared at her, trying to figure out which of the three of her was real.

"The last time we were together was that quickie in your office." Her hands pulled at the hem of his t-shirt. "That had to be two weeks ago."

The air-conditioning brushed against Cobra's bare chest and mixed with the warmth of her tongue as she traced the snake tattoo that wound up his neck. He wanted to tell her to stop. He wanted to tell her he wasn't into it.

"I think it's time for us to start over."

Cobra sunk his head into the couch cushions, and let her words float over him.

"Put the past behind us, and do this right." She ran her fingers through his hair. "I'll even forgive you for stepping out with that brunette."

Sheena's face swam through his tequila-soaked brain as

he stared into Patrice's narrowed eyes. "After all, I had you first, and she's no good for you anyway."

Her cold fingers slid over his abs and when he shifted her hand fell to the sofa. "You never had me," Cobra challenged.

"You know what I mean. Running the club, dealing with Vinnie, especially dealing with Vinnie."

His brain clicked at the mention of Vinnie's name. "You should stay far away from that fucker."

"Him and I are strictly business. He was just playing his usual mind games before, but I told him I would take care of everything."

"Like me?" Cobra's street sense filtered through the flood of tequila.

"Like us." She stated the words so clearly that his brain froze, remembering when he'd used the word *us* to refer to him and Sheena. How she'd challenged him, almost as scared as him to make a commitment.

"But don't worry, I have it all under control." Patrice's bright pinpointed eyes shone against the dim light of the room. "I knew she was in your apartment that morning, but I forgive you."

Her words jogged him out of his tequila haze. Forgive him. He didn't do anything that needed forgiving. He struggled to a standing position and nabbed his t-shirt off the couch.

"What are you doing?"

"Getting the hell outta here." He tugged his t-shirt over his head, and keywords from Patrice rang through his head and set off a loud fuckin' alarm.

"You two almost had me." He stood over her, his vision miraculously clear. Seeing the two-faced bitch for what she was. A gold digger playing both sides of the fence, ready to fuck the highest bidder.

"What two?"

"You and Vinnie. Working me. Controlling me. What better way for him to set me up than to use his number one whore."

Funny how it never bothered him before. It was easy to accept fake until you got it real. He definitely had to get shit straight with Sheena.

He headed for the door and she grabbed his arm and spun him around. "You're wrong. I wanted you. I would be good for you."

"Be careful what you wish for, baby."

"You stupid, dumb thug." Bitter anger replaced the syrupy sweetness of her voice. "You should be happy that a woman like me even looked at you."

He laughed, mocking her with his smile. "There's the bitch. I knew she'd come out to play."

She pushed against his chest, fire in her eyes, her lips twisted into an ugly sneer. "You think you're so smart, but you're making a huge mistake. You better tell that little cunt to be careful because she's not going to be able to save you. She may not even be able to save herself."

Cobra's hand flew to Patrice's jaw. He squeezed just enough to send a message. His voice low and laced with venom. "Don't ever threaten her or you'll find out exactly what kinda thug I am." He ripped his hand away from her face and pulled on the door.

"Fuck you," she screamed. "You'll be sorry you did this 'cause that bitch played you."

He heard the door slam, but he kept going down the hall and then into the stairwell. Being with Patrice was like lighting a cigarette with a blow torch. Overkill and way too much trouble.

When he reached the first floor he braced his hand against

the metal door, then pushed through to the rear of the club. His breath heaved in and out, as Patrice's words echoed in his brain. Sheena had played him and he fuckin' fell for it. They were all working together and that was fucked up on any level.

He was too wasted to drive and he didn't feel like calling Python and listening to him tell him what an asshole he was. The lumpy couch in his office was his only answer. He'd lay down, sleep it off, then head home.

He flipped on the light, pulled his t-shirt over his head, then flopped down on the too small couch and balled the t-shirt under his head. Tomorrow he'd put all this bullshit behind him. Vinnie tried to push his buttons, but the facts remained. Sheena lied to him, and lies could get him killed. Tomorrow, when he was thinking straight, he'd find out exactly what she was about and get the true story out of her.

WHEN THEY WERE HALFWAY to Ecstasy Sheena decided to look down at herself. Probably should've assessed her outfit before they left Daisy's condo, but no, in typical bad luck fashion Sheena had on the same jeans and t-shirt she'd been in all day.

"Why didn't you suggest I change my clothes before we did this?" Sheena cut a glance to Daisy.

"You look fine." Daisy dismissed her worry with a wave of her hand.

"I look like I've been riding on the back of a motorcycle for almost four hours, most of it through the dry, dusty Nevada desert."

"He's a biker, he'll love it."

Sheena gripped the wheel tighter, debating on making the detour to her apartment and changing or just soldiering on.

"I guess I should've given you something of mine, but really you look—"

Sheena's loud laugh cut her off. "Right, like the clothes that fit your model thin body would fit me."

At five foot seven, she doubted that Daisy weighed more than one hundred and twenty pounds. She had a ravenous appetite and never put on an ounce—something Sheena could easily hate her for, if she didn't love her like a sister.

"You can put yourself down all you want, but from what you told me Cobra loves your curves."

True. He had mentioned her hips and ass on numerous occasions. Of course, in comparison to his bulk—

"If I remember correctly you told me he said you were petite."

"Have you seen the man? A rhinoceros would seem petite next to him."

"Stop putting yourself down. I wish my hair was half as thick as yours and your lips are amazing."

Sheena raised her hand off the wheel and held it up. "Now that just sounds weird."

"All true. You're a beautiful, sexy woman and when we find his sorry ass up to his elbows in paperwork, in his office, nursing a beer, you're going to tell him how you feel. And then you're going to tell me how right I was."

Sheena drew in a deep breath as she steered the car into Ecstasy's parking lot. She avoided the valet parking sign and headed toward self-parking, reasoning that she would have the car keys for a quick getaway if needed.

Okay, they were here but the neon multi-colored sign advertising Ecstasy—Where Dreams Come True, and then an outline of a curvy silhouette kind of freaked her out. One

because her dreams never came true, and two because
—Really?

"Did you come here to sit in the car?" Daisy's impatient tone broke her out of her moment of dread.

"We're really doing this, huh?"

"You're really doing this, yes."

"For someone who drank almost an entire bottle of wine you're very pushy and remarkable sharp," Sheena said.

Daisy squeezed her arm. "I just want to see my best friend get what she deserves."

"Oh God, don't say that. If we all got what we deserved . . ."

"All right, so maybe a bad choice of words, but you know what I mean." Daisy leaned in a gave her a hug. "Now, c'mon let's do this." Then she laughed. "I've seen you walk in on million-dollar cons with less fear."

Sure, because running a con was a fake persona. This was real and raw and putting her feelings out there. When she ran a con she hid behind the disguise. Now she was wide open, all out there, free falling—She had to stop.

"Let's do this." Sheena pushed the car door open with more force than necessary.

Luck was in her favor. Apparently, Sunday was ladies night, no cover.

"Nice, at least if things go to shit, it didn't cost us anything," Sheena said into Daisy's ear over the thumping music.

The inside was actually very different than she expected. Leather upholstered booths, hi-gloss wood grain flooring and an enormous curved bar against the far wall. There were different height stages scattered throughout the room with a main stage in the center. And even though the place was packed, the air smelt clean and fresh, an astonishing feat of filtration since smoking was obviously allowed.

Even the girls were classy. Each had a theme costume, but they were all beautiful. Nothing sleazy here. And yes she was standing in the middle of a strip club but knowing that Cobra ran what seemed to be a high-end, exclusive establishment made her feel better about him as a person.

They weaved their way to the main bar. A few men eyeballed them, probably wondering why they had so many clothes on. Since most of the men were around the stages, the bar was relatively quiet. A tall, thin beauty with waist length blonde hair and a name tag that read Clarissa smiled waiting for their order.

Sheena leaned into the bar. "I'm looking for Cobra."

Clarissa paused for a second longer than normal and Sheena added. "I'm a friend of his." Shit, that sounded lame. Why was she explaining herself?

"Last I saw he was headed toward the offices." She pointed to the rear of the room.

"Thanks."

"She said he's by the offices," she told Daisy.

"What did I tell you?" Daisy said as they stayed along the perimeter of the room where it was less crowded. "He's in his office doing paper work." They weaved around some tables off to the side with reserved signs on them and found a wide rear hallway that contained the restrooms and Sheena assumed the offices.

She felt a little awkward just barging into his office and what if there was more than one office. She stopped suddenly and stared down the hallway at a familiar face. The same woman she'd seen at Cobra's penthouse, the one Cobra called Patrice, just exited one of the rooms on the far left. She'd certainly know who and where Cobra might be and since

Patrice had never seen her, it would just seem like an innocent question, right?

"You look lost, hun. Can I help you?" Patrice asked.
Problem solved.

"I'm looking for Cobra."

"Really? You mind me asking what for?"

"Just need to speak to him."

"Well," she giggled. A most annoying sound. "We've
been doing a little partying and he's a little out of it."

Sheena's tongue stuck to the roof of her mouth.

Patrice flung her arm in the direction of the room she just
exited. "You can check it out for yourself, but I don't think
he's up to talking."

Daisy stormed past Patrice down the hall leaving Sheena
staring blankly at this tall, horribly perfect specimen of a
woman, whom she wanted to kill.

Then Sheena's feet moved her forward against her will.
She should've turned and walked the other way. She
should've let Daisy assess the damages and then refuse to
hear about it. But of course, she didn't. In a true testament to
Sheena's fucked up love life she stumbled into the office,
while Daisy ripped a very out of it Cobra a new asshole.

Sheena stared in a daze at Cobra sprawled out on the
couch, shirtless, one leg hanging off the couch, with his arm
flung over his eyes, drunk or high, or both. Maybe sex with
Patrice was so potent that it hurled him into a sex coma. The
smeared lipstick on his neck and chest drove a dagger
through her stomach. She jerked her head away, not wanting
to see or imagine where else Patrice's lips had traveled.

Sheena backed out of the room and stood dumbly in the
doorway until Daisy finished her rant. Bits and pieces filtered
through her nightmare. Fucking asshole, fucking jerk, fucking
bastard. It all centered on the same theme.

At one point Cobra struggled to sit up then shielded his eyes like Daisy's barrage blinded him, but that only made Daisy yell louder, causing Cobra to shrink into the couch cushions. For a split-second Sheena actually felt sorry for him, but that quickly passed when she pictured him screwing Patrice on that couch, in this very room.

Daisy waved her arms around, huffed out a breath, turned on her heel, and hooked her arm into Sheena's. "We're out of here."

As Daisy pulled Sheena's numb self through the club and toward the front door, a very limber and ambitious redhead did a slow back bend to a seductive version of the Rolling Stones *You Can't Always Get What You Want* and the irony was not lost on Sheena. Although Mick and the boys probably didn't know when they wrote the hit song how apropos it would be for her on this night in this strip club.

Not only couldn't she get what she wanted, she couldn't even get what she needed. Her life was far more screwed up than any rock and roll song and although her mind automatically spit out sass, her heart was breaking. The damage was done.

The whole time in Daisy's condo and then on the ride to Ecstasy Sheena hoped against hope that this time would be different. Daisy's encouraging words spurred her on, but even Daisy was silent now.

They pulled out of Ecstasy's lot in silence and when Daisy turned in her seat to say something, Sheena held up her hand. "Please, don't."

"I just want to say how—"

"How sorry you are. I know. It's fine. I'll be fine."

Sheena gripped the wheel and concentrated on the road in front of her because this time she didn't think she would be fine.

CHAPTER SEVENTEEN

He'd died and gone to hell. That was the only explanation for the pounding in Cobra's head, the stinging of his eyes and the absolute dryness of his mouth. The fiery inferno had burned out his eyes and dried out his mouth. Yeah, that made fuckin' sense. Not.

He slowly pried his eyes open, then squeezed them shut. Shit, the whole damn room was spinning like an out of control amusement park ride. He laid perfectly still but he knew if he didn't get up he'd fry in this nightmare. Either that or piss himself 'cause right now his dick felt like it was going to burst.

He edged up on his elbows keeping his eyes half closed against the light. Little by little he rotated his head. What the hell was he doing in his office at Ecstasy? He sucked in a deep breath and tried to concentrate, tried to recall how he got here and better yet why his shirt was off and crumbled under his head.

A tequila bottle on its side made a nasty puddle alongside the couch, and the smell had his intestines twisting around his stomach. He angled his body into a sitting position and at least the room stopped spinning. What the hell did he do last night?

He came here to see Vinnie, they fought and then he sat at the bar with—Patrice. He squeezed his eyes shut and forced himself to concentrate, but nothing. Sitting at the bar was the last clear vision he could recall. That and a dream about Joker's wife, Daisy, screaming shit at him. How crazy was that?

Blackout Fuckin' Drunk. It'd been a long time since he got this trashed. Not only did it screw with his body, but it wasn't safe or smart for the president of the Serpents to be out of control. Drugs and alcohol were a one-way ticket to the graveyard and an open door for your enemies to take over.

He leaned forward resting his head in his hands and tried to focus on his conversation with Vinnie, but all he got were bits and pieces.

A door slammed, his head jerked up and he swore to fuck that he saw stars.

"It's always the last place you look." Python gave him the once over. "Shit man, you look like hell."

Cobra massaged his temples but Python glaring at him sure didn't help.

"Called and texted a few times but . . ."

Cobra patted his pockets, then ran his hand along the couch and found his phone between the cushions. "Dead."

"I was starting to think maybe Vinnie smoked your ass. I sent Rattler over to your penthouse. The only place left was here—Or a hundred miles out in the desert. You can't keep doin' these disappearing acts."

"Yeah, yeah, I know." The last thing he needed right now was another lecture from Python about his duties as club president.

"I'm getting tired of looking for you and trying to figure out where you're at."

Cobra slowly raised his head. "I get it. As president I should always be available and I've been dropping the ball lately, but as my Sargent at Arms you should know when to keep your damn mouth shut. Does that cover everything."

Cobra grunted his response. Good enough.

"I'll give you a thousand bucks if you make me a cup of coffee." Cobra scrubbed his hands over his face.

Python headed for the coffee maker on the counter in the corner. "What the hell happened?" Python said as he set up the coffee.

Wasn't that the million-dollar question. "Fuck if I know. I remember telling Vinnie our deal was over. He said shit, I said shit . . . and then I was sitting at the bar getting smashed."

A few minutes later, Python handed him a steaming cup of black coffee staring like he was waiting for some great revelation as to why his president got drunk off his ass.

"What did he say to get you so twisted up?"

Cobra sipped the hot, black liquid hoping it would do something for his memory.

"I came in to Ecstasy and Vinnie and Patrice were hugged up at the bar. Typical dick move on his part, but I brushed it off. Then we sat down and I told him we were through with all his shit at the weed farm and the underage girls. He knew we hired the DR's to do the heist on his games. And he admitted to calling the cops. Apparently, we weren't supposed to walk outta there. He didn't plan on the DR's fighting back or us having enough fire power to save our asses."

"All right, that's fucked up, but us being threatened is nothing new."

Python was right, they got threats all the time from rival clubs, guys looking to take over their territory, but no it was more than that, this was—shit Vinnie had threatened Danny.

"The night is still hazy." Even Python didn't know about Danny. He'd kept his brother a secret all these years to protect him. A lot of good that did him.

"It must've been pretty fucked up."

Threatening Danny went over the limit, but his memory taunted him with more. Something just out of reach.

"I got some interesting news too." Python sipped at his coffee. "The president of the Renegades in Chicago reached out. Seems the Chicago mob they're associated with isn't too happy with Vinnie either. He said Vinnie's been skimming off the top and not giving them what's owed. Probably why he's coming down hard on us. He's behind and he can't catch up."

"Fuckin' bastard." Cobra put his mug on the coffee table, then patted his pockets for his smokes. "Instead of being happy with the take, he got greedy."

"Might just work in our favor. If Chicago ain't happy, probably means the boys on the East Coast ain't happy either. More allies for us."

Cobra stayed silent. East Coast mob? Looking something up on Wiki?

"What's the matter?" Python asked.

"Something else Vinnie said—Fuck, it's so hazy. He said he knew a secret . . ."

He tried to retrieve it, tried to—Oh shit, Vinnie told him Sheena's real name. Told him she was connected to a mob family in Jersey. He looked it up on Wiki and it was all there, clear and concise. His heart stuttered as it all came back. Sheena was working for Vinnie, Sheena set him up for the hit, Sheena was conning him all along.

"A secret about who?" Python leaned against the desk examining him.

"I can't remember." Cobra pushed himself off the couch. "I gotta take a piss."

Piece by piece Vinnie's revelation haunted him, but he'd keep that to himself.

First he'd make a call to Brookdale and tell the staff that Danny was to get no visitors except him until further notice, then he'd find out the truth about the mob princess.

TWENTY-FOUR HOURS WASN'T a long time when compared to years, decades, centuries, but to Sheena the seconds and minutes of this last day seemed endless. Daisy wanted to stay with her after they left Ecstasy. She even called Joker and yelled at him about what an asshole Cobra was being. Poor Joker.

In the end, Sheena told Daisy to go home. She appreciated her friend's loyalty even if it was misplaced, but Sheena had to face facts. Cobra regretted talking about a future relationship with her. Then that same night went to his longtime girlfriend, further cementing the fact that he and Sheena were done.

None of this was hearsay. She saw it with her own eyes. No gossip, no second-hand information. The truth and the facts hit her square in the face.

HE'S JUST NOT THAT INTO YOU!

She dragged herself through the next day and even made it to her shift at the Pirate's Cove. One ray of sunshine. Seth was off. Saving her from looking at yet another failed relationship.

Now, she laid tucked into her bed in her tiny apartment

willing her exhausted body to fall asleep. Thankfully, sleep always came easy to her, like a magic elixir she could call upon when needed.

As her eyes drifted shut, she heard a noise. She dismissed it, blaming it on the air conditioning. She shifted, rearranged her pillow and a hand clamped down over her mouth.

"Don't move."

An overwhelming fear jetted through her. Yes, she could defend herself. On the street, not lying flat on her back in bed, dressed in her sleep t-shirt and sweat pants. She twisted her body, but the hand pushed her head further into the pillow. Her blackout shades allowed no light or shadows.

"Don't scream when I lift my hand, or you'll regret it." The harsh rasp was eerily familiar, but no.

The pressure over her mouth eased, but her assailants body hovered above her. His weight shifted, her bedside lamp switched on and she gasped.

The hard, tough face that loomed over her scared her. Raw, gut searing fear. Not an emotion she usually experienced. Her eyes shifted to the gun firmly gripped in his left hand. She swallowed hard, her mind scamming for a way out of this disastrous situation.

"How long did you think you could fool me?" He leaned closer, letting her see his fierce anger—and pain? Her nostrils flared and inhaled the scent of leather, smoke and male. Cobra.

She shifted again and he pushed her into the bed with the flat of his palm firmly planted on her chest.

"What are you doing? Why are you here?" she whispered.

"I came for the truth." He eased up on the bed. One booted foot firmly on the floor, the other leg bent with his knee on the mattress digging against her hip.

"How did you get in—"

His sarcastic glare cut her off. "Your locks are crap. Shit easy to bust."

For a split second she considered she was dreaming this bizarre scenario, but the gun only inches from her vital organs made it all too real.

"Why don't you let me get up, and we'll talk." She used her calm, placating the crazy person voice. It usually worked in the past. Irate marks, guys on the run—

He grabbed her bicep, and suddenly she was standing by the edge of the bed. The man's strength and power floored her. He eyeballed her for a second, then ordered, "Put on shoes. You're coming with me."

"I'm not going anywhere until you tell me what's going on." She would've liked to put her hands on her hips in a firm stance of rebellion, but he still had hold on her upper arm.

"Here's how this is gonna go. You're gonna put shoes on, and get on my bike." He pulled her flush against his hard body. "You're not gonna fight me, and you're not gonna cause any trouble."

She drew in a breath to protest and he cut her off.

"You're gonna do exactly as I say Serena Victoria Cipriani."

Her heart skidded to a stop. Then pumped hard and deep. Weakness combined with amped up fear jolted through her body. She responded to her given name by nodding.

He released her and she retrieved her low boots.

"We're gonna be on my bike for forty minutes so go to the bathroom now 'cause I ain't making any stops."

She did her business then they wordlessly left her apartment. The still, warm night air surrounded them as they descended the concrete and metal stairs from her second-floor apartment. The small, two-story complex formed a rectangle around a pool. Similar to many of the low-budget residences that dotted the area off Flamingo. Most of the tenants were service people for the casinos who worked shifts all hours of the day and night. Finding someone swimming at two in the morning wasn't unusual, but tonight the pool and surrounding area was vacant.

To anyone watching they looked like just another couple. No one could see the outline of the large silver gun stuck into the waist of his jeans, or the grim expression on his face while he led her to his Harley parked at the curb.

He handed her a helmet. "Don't get any ideas about jumping off my bike or any other kind of bullshit."

His glare sent a warning, but honestly she was relieved. The charade was finally over.

He stood over her until she mounted the bike then threw his leg over the wide seat. By the time they drove through downtown Vegas and hit Route 95 her body was in perfect sync with his. She even fooled herself into thinking that they were just another couple out for a ride on a warm Vegas night.

Nothing compared to riding with Cobra. The wind in her face, the speed, the sensation of being one with the machine rumbling under her, one with Cobra. Erotic, exhilarating and exactly how she shouldn't feel. The man kidnapped her for God's sake.

The ascent on the dark mountain road made her grip his waist tighter, but he clearly had done this trip many times before and knew every twist and turn. She assumed they were headed for the mountain cabin he mentioned when they were at the Grand Canyon.

Her mind briefly revisited that glorious day. How he'd made her feel like she was the only one that existed in the crowded national park. How he'd held her and promised they had a future beyond that day. Then how it all came crashing down in the parking garage. The letdown and the dull pain were so familiar, but she blamed herself for letting his words mean so much to her.

The darkness of the wooded area surrounded them as he slowed the bike and steered them down a steep driveway illuminated by lights and lined on each side by towering pine trees. The lights cast shadows on an A-frame house built over a garage. He stopped, pressed some buttons on his bike, and the garage door opened. He pulled into the two-car garage next to a Range Rover and the lights came on automatically as the door closed behind them.

A house tucked away on a dark, deserted mountain road, with no visible neighbors. The host of this party a totally pissed, muscled, tattooed biker that outweighed her by at least one hundred pounds who woke her at gunpoint.

And yes, she'd been in tight spots before, but this had much more to do with fear of breaking her heart than breaking of bones. Of course, that might happen too, but that was the least of her worries. What could happen tonight was much more serious than a few fractures.

She removed her helmet and examined her surroundings. The same order and neatness she observed at his penthouse presided over the garage. Tools and car or motorcycle parts neatly arranged on shelves. Even the floor was finished in some kind of acrylic covering.

Cobra dismounted the bike, stored their helmets, then stood in front of her. His eyes cold. A depth of detached isolation she'd never seen in him. His sparkling blue eyes had turned icy like a vast tundra, permanently frozen. She shivered from the chilling atmosphere that surrounded her.

He wordlessly tilted his head toward a door and nudged her forward. They climbed the staircase up one flight with him close behind her. The only sound the heavy scuffing of his boots against the wooden stairs.

They entered the second floor and the light automatically came on. The jolting brightness illuminated an open floor plan with a wall of windows that reflected their image against the dark night. And yes he was right, she did look tiny next to him. Probably not the best observation since he'd taken her here against her will, had barely said five words with a deadly expression plastered on his face.

CHAPTER EIGHTEEN

He nudged her further into the room, then pointed to the couch. His silence gnawed at her. Just get this over with. Do freakin' something already. Yell at her, hit her. Although if he laid hands on her she'd be forced to fight back.

"Relax." Again, he read her body language. Crazy and scary.

"I know how to defend myself."

She'd learned some very useful techniques over the years, so let him just try anything. She was ready.

"I'm not gonna fuckin' hit you." He shook his head. "I've done plenty of messed up shit in my life, but to date I've never hit a woman. And I'm not about to start now."

"Good to know." She sat on the edge of the couch, meeting him glare for glare as he stood above her.

Her threats and tough demeanor sounded good, but the reality of her situation towered over her. All pent up, tightly coiled thug. The real-life gangster that messed with the fantasy she'd created for herself. The dream of taming a man that was untamable.

He pulled an overstuffed chair closer and sat. Their knees were only inches from each other. His eyes cold and still. "Talk."

That's a broad statement. What did he want to hear? The weather, sport statistics, tomorrows stock report. Or the way he broke her heart in a single bound.

"I thought breaking into my apartment with a gun was a bit of overkill."

"In my world enemies come in all shapes and sizes. I can't take any chances."

The irrational thought of her as a villain in a DC Comic popped into her head along with an unexplainable urge to laugh causing a giggle to erupt in her throat.

"You think this is funny?"

"No, not really. Sad, crazy, typical of my life, but probably not funny."

"Your sass was cute when I thought you were harmless, now not so much." He shifted forward on the seat.

"Wasn't it you that told me the first time back at the Gold Mine that nobody's harmless?"

He paused, then tilted his head. "Looks like I should've taken my own advice."

"And that's why instead of just coming to my apartment and asking me your questions, you break in and hold me at gunpoint."

"I said I want answers." His low growl vibrated through her. "Like why did you get close to me? Passing yourself off as someone else."

"I legally changed my name to Sheena when I hit Vegas five years ago, so technically I didn't pass myself off as someone else."

"Are you fuckin' kidding me, right now? You had plenty

of chances to tell me. Like lying in bed after I fucked you stupid, or maybe after some of those mind-blowing orgasms."

"Since they were mind-blowing, rational thought probably wasn't an option." Her traitorous brain took her back to his bedroom. The way he commanded her body, the way he'd drawn her out, and made her feel, made her care. The sex was fantastic, but it was the caring that broke her.

"Again with the smart mouth. You gonna deny that shit or the way you played me."

No she couldn't deny it. No one made her feel like that, but she wasn't about to admit it to him. Not now anyway.

"First of all, I didn't play you. No one knows my real name, not even Daisy."

"Another goddamn lie." He slammed his hand against the arm of the chair. "That fucker Vinnie knows all about you. So how does that work if you're not in on something with him?"

"It's complicated." All these years, all the cons she'd run and her secret was safe. The one time she'd let her guard down karma swooped in and bit her in the ass.

His demanding, single-minded questions shook her. The way those beautiful, icy eyes bored through her. Demanding the truth, prying it from the vault where all her hidden emotions lived. How easy it would be to let it all go, to give in and free herself.

He tilted his head, calling bullshit with just a look. "I want the truth out of your mouth. I also want to know what your angle was in the bar that first night. Why you wanted to get into my penthouse and what you were looking for?"

She barked out a hoarse laugh. More sarcastic than humorous. "You've been watching too many Netflix movies. I didn't have an angle that first night, and I wasn't looking for anything in your penthouse."

"Maybe you dealing at that game was a setup to get me to come rescue you so I get smoked in a shootout."

"Or, you sent the Desert Rats knowing I was there, and putting me in the middle of a shootout." She had as many questions as him and she wasn't about to let him get over on her.

"If I did that, then why the hell did I come in guns blazing. I saved your ass that night."

She shrugged. "Right, and maybe that was a setup too."

"Don't twist this shit up, and turn it on me. I read your father's bio on Wiki. Remember, I know who you are."

"Great. Then why all the drama? Just let me go, you don't care about me anyway."

He paused for the extra minute that made her wonder what exactly he was thinking. "Like I said before, I live in a dangerous world where people do fucked up shit because they can. Vinnie's tied to the Chicago and East Coast mob and big surprise, so are you."

He had her there, but he'd never believe that her meeting up at Daisy and Joker's wedding was coincidence.

"I don't believe in coincidences, so spill."

Shit, it was like he could see into her brain. Freaked her out how he did that.

"You're putting two and two together and coming up with three."

"I don't think so. Vinnie sending a beautiful woman in to fuck my brains out and then spy on me is exactly the shit he would pull."

"Beautiful woman, huh?"

"You already know what I think of you, so don't play anymore games with me."

"No, really I don't know. Being with you has pretty much been like riding a roller coaster without a harness. And right now I feel like I'm free falling, so you might need to clarify."

"I don't have anything to explain."

"How about the bitchy brunette, Patrice who manages Ecstasy, cooks you breakfast, but isn't your girlfriend. Yet, she told me she is your girlfriend. Which would explain her coming out of your office the other night after she left a trail of lipstick all over your body."

"What the hell are you talking about?"

He sounded genuinely surprised.

"You at Ecstasy screwing Patrice on the couch in your office. Is that clear enough?"

"You were at Ecstasy?"

Either he was a better actor than she gave him credit for, or he was really confused.

"And I suppose you don't remember Daisy screaming her head off in your office?"

His hard mask cracked for a second, or was she only seeing what she wanted? Fooling herself again.

"Was the sex with Patrice so good that it blew out your memory?"

His eyebrows knitted together. "I didn't have sex with Patrice."

"That's not what she thinks or said."

"She's lying." He threw his hands up. "I walked out on her. Main reason I was sacked out in my office. That and I was too drunk to drive. After Vinnie blew me apart with your real identity the only logical solution was to get fucked up."

What did it matter. The damage was done. No trust on either side, but he did sound convincing. "You were pretty out of it."

"That's what happens when you find out someone that you started to care about was lying to you." He braced his hands on his knees and leaned in. "Especially when the news is delivered by a slimy prick who enjoyed making me twist."

A hint of pain flashed over his face and she clasped her hands together so she couldn't reach out to him.

"So yeah, I got trashed, but I didn't screw Patrice. Her and me were over before we started." He screwed up his lips. "But instead of having faith you believed that lying bitch."

Lies and deceit destroyed whatever they had, but right now she believed him. The timber of his voice, the pain that skittered over his face, but he wasn't blameless either.

"Just like you believed Vinnie when he told you I set you up at the warehouse."

"Completely different. I never hid who I was or what I was about." He narrowed his eyes." The fact remains, you lied about who you are."

"And you fell into Vinnie's trap instead of asking me the real reasons behind my identity change."

"Oh, fuck no. I asked you about what you were hiding the first night we were together, so don't put that on me."

"Maybe I wasn't ready to give up all my secrets." That bastard Vinnie gave it all away. Doing it in a way that sabotaged anything her and Cobra could've had, so why bother. She blew out a long-held breath and sunk into the couch. "You win. I'm done."

Seconds turned into minutes, but his glittering gaze never faltered.

"I'll tell you whatever you want to know, but I wasn't spying on you for Vinnie or anyone else." She sunk deeper into the couch suddenly exhausted. "I was honestly attracted to you at the Gold Mine. No ulterior motive, no agenda. Just plain old-fashioned desire."

THEY'D BEEN FACING each other for almost half an hour. Cobra saw a few different emotions pass over Sheena/Serena's face. Most of her expressions centered around sass and denial and then after all the bullshit she finally admitted it. She followed that up with her feelings about him, and hell yeah, he wanted to believe her.

He could just hear Python and the other guys calling him a pussy. Telling him how stupid he was for falling for her lines again, but he couldn't deny it. He was attracted to her too, and fuck if that didn't scare the shit right out of him.

"Why don't you start at the beginning. Like why you came to Vegas and why you changed your name."

"Fine. You might as well hear my version of it." She pulled at the strings of her pajama pants. "I was born Serena Victoria Cipriani, in Brooklyn, New York. When I was seven we moved to a New Jersey suburb. A six-bedroom McMansion with stone pillars, marble statues, a housekeeper, tennis courts and a waterfall spilling into the Olympic sized pool." She remembered her idyllic childhood with fondness and longing. Wishing it had never changed.

"My life was a normal kid's life. Barbecues in the summer, presents under the tree at Christmas. My brother and I never knew my father was a real-life Tony Soprano. We actually didn't live far from where that was filmed. Everybody was happy, life was good, and then little by little the edges of that life started to fray."

She lowered her head and stared at the wood plank floor.

"Little things at first, like more men around the house than usual. Bodyguards picking us up at school. Power within the organization was shifting, people were getting greedy."

Cobra pressed his palms against his thighs. Pretty clear this story would not have a good ending.

"Everything was coming apart. You asked me how I was

so calm in the gunfight and knew about cleaning up your wound. I'd been doing that since I was a teenager. When there'd be trouble my father would bring his crew to the house to get fixed up. I learned at my mother's side how to clean out knife wounds, even watched my mother dig a bullet out of my father's leg once. As I'm sure you're aware, going to the hospital isn't an option and my mother had studied to be a nurse, then she met my father and never graduated, but she knew enough to get by. People think organized crime, the mob, the Mafia is some magical world, but the fact is it's real people who bleed, scream out in pain and sometimes die. We're all built the same and getting shot or stabbed can end your life no matter who you are or what your name is."

"That's mind-blowing and fucked up at the same time." Every time she opened her mouth she gutted him with her guts.

"Our basement was set up like a mini hospital and because of my father's connections we had quality grade surgical equipment and meds."

"His enemies were looking for any weak link." She mashed her lips together, and drew in a deep breath. "That weak link was my brother. He started using weed in middle school and by high school he'd moved up to coke and whatever else he could smoke, snort and shoot. Everyone from our priest to his numerous counselors had a theory why he did this, but to me the answer was simple. He couldn't live up to my father's expectations; plus, he didn't want to. My brother was artistic, a sensitive soul who hated violence."

Just like his own brother, Danny. The realization rocked Cobra.

"So, your father's enemies used your brother against him."

Her sharp intake of breath told him he was right. They

stared at each other for a long minute and Cobra wasn't sure he wanted her to go on.

"They filled his head with lies and drugs, then one night it all came to a head. I was home on summer break from college and I heard Angelo and my father fighting in his room again. I went in, foolishly thinking I could smooth things over. The fight escalated so fast and all of a sudden, my brother was waving around a gun, yelling and threatening my father. My father tried to reason with him, knowing he was high, but my brother became more unhinged. Making accusations and blaming my father for his drug addiction."

She paused and he sensed her mind working trying to find the right words.

"To an extend, my brother was right, my father lived in a screwed up world, but he was a good Dad, and I know he loved me and my brother."

"Sometimes people do the wrong things for the right reasons." Cobra's whole life in one sentence.

"I stepped to my brother thinking I could talk him down. I grabbed for the gun, we struggled and when my father lunged forward to help me the gun when off, and a second later my father lay dead on my brother's bedroom floor."

Of all the things he expected her to say. That wasn't it. His brain ticked off more questions, but he remained silent.

"No matter what people said about him, he was my father and I loved him."

She raised her hand to her cheek and he pushed it away, then swiped at the fat tear running down her soft skin. When she drew in a shuddered breath it wrecked him. He knew only too well about keeping shit in. Bottling everything up until the pressure pushed against your insides in a desperate struggle to get out.

He drew her to him. She struggled against his hold, but he

only clutched her tighter. He tilted her chin up to meet his gaze—sensing that she didn't want to break away. He slid his forehead against hers, their eyes inches apart. "So, you ran here to escape."

Again, she wriggled in his firm hold, but he had her locked in. One arm wrapped around her shoulders while the other wrapped around her waist, anchored on her ass.

"Not exactly. My brother had so many priors and drug charges by then, he surely would've ended up in prison, so I took the blame and told the police I was holding the gun when it accidentally went off."

"Fuck. That's loyalty."

"I also had some of the highest paid lawyers in the State of New Jersey. People that know people that make things happen, and after two weeks, a mistrial was declared."

"Impressive, but if you got off—"

"I was told it was for my own good. Get out of Jersey and start over. New name, new identity, but really it was about saving face. Me being in Jersey was a constant reminder of the lack of respect from my father's own family. My father had people he answered to and being shot in his home by one of his children made his whole crew look weak.

"They helped me with lawyers and making it all go away, but of course then they expected something in return. Get far away from Jersey and stay far away from Jersey and they would leave my mother and brother alone."

"As fucked up as that sounds, I get it. So, you came out here and then what?" She lowered her head, but he wasn't having it. "Look at me."

"They contacted Vinnie to "look after me" and the rest is history. He was my handler. He expedited the change of my name, hooked me up with Daisy and we dealt his high-end games. Money was good, everything was great until it wasn't.

Vinnie started getting sloppy, taking too much off the top. After one of his partners was indicted for tax evasion, Daisy took off to Miami, met up with Joker, and Seth and I decided to get out of the game."

"Unbelievable. Vinnie screwed you up from the beginning."

"I can't believe how gullible I was, but at twenty-one I was on the run, with only a year and a half of college, and no skills. At the time, I looked at Vinnie like my savior."

"Some savior," Cobra snorted. "What happened to the rest of your family?"

"My mother couldn't adjust. Not so much to the loss of my father, but to the loss of her status and money. There's no mobster pension plan for the widows of gunned down gangsters, so my mother did the next best thing. She hooked up with a low-level bookie and decided shoving large amounts of coke up her nose made everything better."

"And your brother?"

"He's been on a constant merry-go-round of jail, rehab, jail, probation, jail, rehab. I'm just waiting to find out he didn't wake up one morning."

"Sounds like we both got screwed in the family department."

"I liked the anonymity because I had no intentions of Bravo making me the next Victoria Gotti in some skanky reality show."

"Who else knows about you?"

"Just you. And Vinnie, of course."

"Not even Daisy."

"Nope."

Wow, that was some revelation. She'd been in Vegas five years, been through all kinds of cons with Daisy and yet he was the first one to know her story.

"Kinda weird that we never met up before this," Cobra said

"Not really. Vinnie and I always met in the casino bar at the Bellagio. I knew he had other things going on, but I was only involved in the poker games. Then for the last four months I was leading the straight life. My mistake was contacting him again to make some fast money."

"So how come you were dealing at the warehouse on Valley View and not at his high stakes game."

She cocked her head. "Vinnie's way of punishing me for leaving him the first time. He said Seth and I would have to work our way up again."

"Cocksucker. He's all about control."

He examined her closely as she dragged in another deep breath.

"Stop staring at me like you're trying to figure out a puzzle."

"I'm just taking it all in."

"Taking it in as in 'you don't believe me,' or taking it in as in 'how can I get away from her?' Believe me, I know what my last name stands for, I know the usual reaction. I've seen it all. Fear, hate. People wanting to be with me because of my family and people shunning me because of my family." Her voice rose and she flailed her arms around and pushed against him, her eyes blazing with sad disappointment. "I came to realize that there are no real reactions, no real feelings, just people's preconceived ideas of how I should look and act."

"Babe." Cobra shook her shoulders with enough force to snap her out of her crazy. "Calm the hell down."

"No, you don't understand. You see me as I am now, but when I first got here I was lonely and scared. I'd been on trial for a crime I didn't commit. My mother and brother were no help. Half the time they never even showed up at the court-house. Luckily, I was released, but within days I was shipped out here and put in Vinnie's very incapable hands." She collapsed against him. "It's just that . . ."

"No baby, I get it." He cradled her head against his shoulder. His gaze drifted over her shoulder to the dark night. He'd brought her here with the intention of scaring the truth out of her. He'd gotten the truth, then saw another side of this brave woman who was weaving her way into his life. So many tried to get close to him, get inside of him, and yet Sheena's honesty was so real and raw it hurt.

He saw now that her sass and quick tongue were a way of closing herself off, protecting herself. The only weapon available to shield her from the hurt caused by so many others. He thought his past was fucked up, but she'd done nothing to deserve the shit that was thrown at her except being born into the wrong family.

CHAPTER NINETEEN

Cobra eased away from her and she slumped against the couch pillows. Her story exhausted her. For five years she'd held in the truth and while it was liberating to finally get it all out, the reliving of that horrible day and the weeks that followed her father's death flooded her with renewed guilt. The actions she should've taken, the words she should've said. It all came tumbling back, choking her with regret.

Cobra eased next to her, gaging her emotions and somehow sensing her fragile state. The same outlaw biker who broke into her apartment, held her at gunpoint and drove her to his cabin hideaway now stared at her with a compassion that she'd never experienced.

Most of her life she'd worried about her mother and her brother, and even her father when she was old enough to realize what his life represented. Not once had anyone ever worried about her. They let her take the blame for a murder she'd tried to prevent and then shipped her two thousand miles away.

He held out a tumbler of amber liquid. "Take a sip, you need it."

She brought the heavy, etched glass to her lips peering at him while she drank deep knowing a sip wouldn't be enough. Her eyes watered and a little gasp choked her throat.

"I told you to sip. That's twenty-year-old bourbon."

She swallowed a few times, then wiped at her eyes. "I have a hard time following direction."

"No, shit. And you're also stubborn as fuck."

"Oh great. Is this the part where we compliment each other?" She waved her hand dramatically around the room. "Because I have to say, for a kidnapper you have very nice taste."

"Always with the sass."

She brought the glass to her lips again and this time she sipped. "We have to be the two most screwed up people on the planet."

"I was just thinking that."

"Who else rips someone out of their bed after midnight against their will, holds them captive, then serves them high end liquor?"

"Gotta admit, this thing we got goin' is kinda fucked up."

"I'm almost afraid to ask. Is this the norm with you and a woman, or have you saved all your crazy for me?"

He threw his head back and laughed. "You say the goddamn funniest things." He brought his laughter under control and his face sobered. "First truth. I don't share this bourbon with anyone. Second truth. You're the only woman I've ever brought up here."

That revelation blew all her flip replies right out of her head.

"Finally shut ya up. For once you don't have some smart-ass remark."

"That is pretty shocking. Not even sharing that bourbon with Python?" She waggled her eyebrows teasing him, totally ignoring his other revelation.

"Don't be a smart ass, you heard the second part of that."

And she was surprised to say the least, but seeing this more private side of him made sense too. He wasn't a man who shared easily, and she sensed there was something he was still holding back from her.

"I heard you and I'm honored."

In a flash he grabbed the glass and set it on the coffee table, then dug his hand into her hair. "I know one sure way to prove it to you."

His crystal blue eyes darkened like the summer sky at dusk. He drew her closer with one hand around her waist while his other hand tugged on her hair to expose her neck. He nibbled her ear and the sweet spot just behind her ear. Her soft moan made him suck harder, then travel down the column of her neck until she shivered in anticipation.

A few minutes ago, her stomach was twisted with regret and remorse, but now it hummed. Like Cobra himself administered a magic elixir that spread through her body and smoothed out all the rough edges.

How could a man she wanted to hate and tear apart not twenty minutes ago light her up and set her on fire. The feelings and emotions she experienced with him were so new and foreign that she didn't know where to put them. Like going from zero to sixty on a racetrack with no parachute to stop you from hitting the inevitable brick wall.

He leaned away from her. "You're doin' way too much thinking."

"How do you do that? Read my mind."

"It's a gift. I can do it with my enemies too. Anytime my

senses are wired." He flashed her a sly grin. "And you get me all amped up."

"When we first got here I was so pissed at you."

"And now?"

When she stayed quiet he leaned in and laved the little bites he'd made on her neck. "So sweet," he mumbled against her skin.

"Now, I want what I know I can't have, what I know will be bad for me."

He twisted his lips into a smirk. "Don't be so cryptic, babe. Spit it out. We're shit bad for each other, but damn it all to hell I can't keep away from you and from the looks of it you got it bad for me too."

"Hmm, like the moth to the flame, the match to the fire and whatever other cliché you can come up with."

"More like a fuckin' bomb to a wild fire."

"The truth is we are destined for disaster."

He scooped her up and the next thing she knew they were off the couch and headed for the stairs of the loft. Never ceased to amaze her how he flipped her around like a feather. "So, if we're gonna go up in flames we might as well enjoy it and burn together."

His heavy boots clomped up the stairs and into the open area above the main floor.

She squeaked when he tossed her onto the bed, then she propped herself up on her elbows. No way she was missing the show of this beautiful man taking off his clothes.

A cocky grin appeared when he realized her eyes were on him, then he teased her by slowly pulling his shirt off over his head. That sight alone was orgasmic.

"Before this night is over you are going to tell me what every one of those tattoos mean."

"Deal." He flung the shirt at her and she caught it midair.

His long fingers hovered over the button of his jeans, pausing, testing her. She wanted to jump forward and speed up the process but this was his show and they were both enjoying it.

"You're very good at this. Maybe you should try out for Chippendales on the Strip."

"Nah, I only want one lady looking at what I have to offer."

After more agonizing seconds he inched his zipper down exposing that glorious Ride Till I Die tat.

She pointed to his abs. "You still haven't told me the meaning behind that."

"No, I haven't." He leaned into her, his palms planted on the bed, his pants hanging off his hips , and she didn't care that he didn't answer her. His body and total attention were focused on her. Like the whole room could burst into flames and all he would see was her. Fire even described their cliched analysis of their relationship.

"Fuck!" His eyes darted to the nightstand. "I don't have any condoms."

"You don't?" she squeaked out.

"Like I said, I don't bring women here so, no."

"I'm on the pill," she said. "And I've been tested."

"I'm clean too. Just got tested before we met."

"You're okay with not using a condom?" Even though she was on the pill, this was a huge step.

"Okay with taking the woman I care about raw. Yeah, I'm good." He anchored his thumbs in the bottom of her sweats and with one jerk she was naked. He nodded to her top. "Take it off."

She leaned up and stripped off her thin sleep shirt.

"Fuckin' perfect." He licked his lips. "There's two things I've been thinking about doin' since I first saw you at the

Gold Mine." He ran his calloused hand down her thigh and she shivered. "I wanted to sink my hand into that thick hair of yours while I take you hard from behind. Maybe even slap that beautiful ass of yours a few times."

A light headedness surged through her and she realized she'd been holding her breath. He did dirty talk so well.

"That was what you were thinking about?"

"Sure as fuck was." He stroked himself letting his hand slide up and down his shaft torturously slow. "Twisting that hair around my fist with one hand and squeezing that ass with the other. Perfect damn fantasy that's about to come true."

Right now, he had her so hot that she didn't care about what happened in the future, the past, or the next hour as long as she had this man near her, in her and on top of her.

COBRA STROKED his cock a few times loving the way her eyes followed his hand like she couldn't wait to get her lips around him. He'd better dial it down a bit or he'd be coming in his own hand.

"Get up on your knees." The rough rasp in his voice gave away his need and he didn't care. He wanted her to know what she did to him. He wanted to show her how she made him feel.

She flipped over and when she popped that perfectly round ass in the air he caressed it with both hands. She peeked over her shoulder at him and damn if she didn't look like a dream come true. Her wild, curly hair draped over her face, full lips parted and dark eyes overflowing with desire.

He gripped her hips and nestled himself between those luscious ass cheeks. He jerked his hips a few times as she ground against him. Best fuckin' sensation ever. He'd be happy to do this all night, and he knew what waited for him, but he wanted to savor every inch of her first. He bent down and traced his tongue up her spine. Fuck, if she didn't arch her back like a cat. Straining to meld with him, to relieve the tension.

He wrapped his arm around her waist and lifted her, then nuzzled his face into her hair. Flowers, the sweet smell of vanilla, and desert air surrounded him. He bit the lobe of her ear and she moaned out, pressing her ass into his rock-hard dick.

"I got you, baby. You never have to worry about anything else, ever." He kissed the side of her neck and she turned her lips to him. He kept the kiss sweet and gentle, wanting her to believe his words and know that from here on she was his and only his.

She tried to deepen the kiss and he broke away. "You get what I'm saying?" he mumbled against her lips.

She nipped at his lower lip, rocking against him.

Hard to ignore what she was doing, but he had to be sure. "You understand that you're mine now." He cupped her chin with his other hand. "Say it. Say the words." His voice came off rough and demanding, but he had to hear it.

"I'm yours," she whispered.

"And no more secrets."

"No more secrets." She devoured his mouth and he lost himself as their tongues teased and twisted. He turned off the part of his brain that said he still had one secret left to tell. Danny. He would tell her about him tomorrow and maybe telling someone would relieve his own guilt. He doubted it, but having her in his corner could chase away some of his demons.

She ground against him again pulling him out of his remorse. Hotter than hell. His heart beat faster in anticipation and then his fingers found her desire, stroking her until she moaned out. He gripped her hips angling for the right position, then slid home.

"Ohh, hell, yeah." This is where he needed to be.

He smoothed his hand up her back and she did that feline move again making him pound into her harder. When his hand reached her hair, he dug in and wrapped those gorgeous curls around his fist and twisted until he captured her lips again.

"You feel that, baby. That's me giving you everything I got."

He nipped at her lips, picking up the pace. His very fantasy coming true in living color. Fuckin' his woman raw, one hand on her ass and the other fisting her hair. Didn't get much better than this.

CHAPTER TWENTY

Sheena wiggled her ass so Cobra hit just the right spot. But with Cobra there was no wrong spot. This man knew exactly what her body needed when it needed it. When he fisted her hair she moaned into his mouth, loving the way he surrounded her, stretched her and made her feel alive.

The telling of her story freed a tight spring of tension that she'd carried around for so long. A burden that weighed her down with guilt and underlying fear. She'd gotten so used to the pressure that the release filled her with an unfamiliar buoyancy. She could definitely enjoy this carefree happiness.

As if sensing her new freedom, he pulled her to him. Her back to his front. Two people in perfect unison. She braced her hand against his headboard.

"Every time, it gets better and better," he growled against her ear. He palmed her ass and gave it a slap. Without a word he brought his palm down again, a bit harder. She gasped as a fire lit in the pit of her belly. His big hand rubbed over the heated skin, massaging and squeezing, then slapping it again.

Her body reacted and when his fingers slipped over her hip and down to her clit she shivered.

"Fuck, baby, you're soaked." His deep rumble was a cross between a growl and a moan. "You like my hand on you, huh?"

She answered by wiggling her ass at him. "God, yes." The glorious pressure built within her, bringing her even higher, and when his fingers found her clit again her head dropped between her shoulders. He teased her spot with a light touch. Not near enough what she needed.

She ground down against him and he lessened the pressure. "Oh, Cobra," she cried out slapping both hands against the headboard, pushing harder.

"What's the matter, babe?" His devilish lilt egged her on.

"Give me what I need," she ground out.

Little dots of sweat ran between her breasts. This man was killing her one second at a time.

"Tell me. Tell me what you need."

She dropped her hand over his and pushed at his fingers to go faster, harder.

"Ahh, is that the way you want it?" He flicked her hand away.

"Yes, yes." She arched her spine needing to feel his fingers in just the right spot. "I need them right there."

Cobra groaned into her neck. His chest slapping against her back, driving deep within her with his glorious cock while his fingers danced over her clit. It was too much and not enough all at the same time. The painful ecstasy of getting what you want and not wanting it to end.

He pulled halfway out settling his cock between her ass cheeks, then thrust back in as his thumb pinched her clit.

"Cobra, ahhhh, so fuckin' good." Her body exploded around his cock and his fingers, but he wasn't done with her yet. Both hands went to her hips and he pounded relentlessly through her aftershocks and then the unbelievable happened.

Her body released again and then again. She panted through the uncontrollable orgasms as they hit her over and over.

He finally stilled, his ragged breathing against her neck, her hands braced against the headboard for support seconds before they collapsed onto the mattress. He rolled them to their side and spooned her gently, caressing her hip.

"You okay?" he asked and she couldn't contain another sigh of contentment. If she were a cat she'd be purring.

"Much better than okay." She covered his hand with hers and turned so they were facing each other. She ran her hand over the side of his face. Loving the extremes of smooth skin and rough stubble. So like him. Gentle and caring, yet strong and tough when needed.

One week ago they celebrated Daisy and Joker's wedding. He'd rescued her from a shootout with the cops and a rival gang, made her walk on a glass floor thousands of feet in the air, then kidnapped her in the middle of the night. Not the usual first dates, but then neither of them was first date material. Nobody would be writing an article under The Guide to First Dates or How We Met in *Bride's Magazine.*

"What are you thinking about?" He pulled the sheet over them and propped some pillows under their heads.

"How crazy everything's been, but also how I wouldn't have wanted it any other way."

"If you like crazy, then we're the perfect pair, baby."

She snuggled into him and noticed the room for the first time. The bed was huge with distressed logs for a headboard, a rustic armoire and a huge TV on the opposite wall. Wooden shades covered the windows, but traces of light seeped through.

"What time is it?"

Cobra shifted and retrieved his phone off the nightstand. "Five a.m."

She stretched and raised her arms over her head. "I feel almost weightless and so relaxed." She grinned at him. "Must be those multiple orgasms."

"You caught me. That's my plan. Keeping you fuck-drunk and happy."

"Fuck-drunk, huh? I think I like the sound of that."

He cuddled her to him. "Sleep for a while, then I'll make you breakfast and we'll eat it out on the porch."

"That sounds wonderful." Her eyes were closing as the words left her mouth, and then a soft tranquility surrounded her.

SHEENA ROLLED over and flung her arm out over the cool sheets. Her eyes fluttered open and shards of light played across the bed. She snuggled deeper into the bedding, loving the way the soft sheets caressed her naked body.

A barrage of visions flooded her brain. Cobra carrying her up the stairs, laying her on the bed, stripping for her. Oh yes, that was magnificent, but then there was the main event. The sex. She was hardly a virgin, but the sensations that man put on her body were sinful and oh so . . . dangerous. So many emotions she'd felt for the first time and multiple orgasms. Her brain halted and stuttered over that one. Sadly, one orgasm was a miracle with most men she'd been with, no less more than one. Unbelievable, outrageous and just plain fucking wonderful.

Her naughty daydream was interrupted by the delicious smell of coffee and mountain air. She'd never been up to Mount Charleston before. Another first. But she knew it was where many Las Vegas residents escaped when the summer heat became unbearable. On any given day the temperature was anywhere from ten to thirty degrees cooler, and on this May morning a chill seeped through Sheena's naked body.

She hated to leave her warm cocoon, but the smell of coffee and whatever else Cobra was cooking didn't give her much of a choice.

She crept out of the warmth of the bed, shivered violently, then made a valiant search for her t-shirt and sweats. She couldn't remember if she'd lost them on the way to the bedroom, or if they were still in the tangle of bedsheets.

Either way she was naked and freaking freezing. A quick rummage through some of his discarded clothes on a chair resulted in a long sleeved, black sweatshirt that fell to her knees with the words Kick Ass or Go Home emblazoned in red across the front.

She slipped into the en suite bathroom, splashed some water on her face and since he'd stolen her out of her bed, there was no makeup smearing her face. Thank God for small favors. She ran her wet hands through her hair and was able to tame the wildest curls and settle them around her head.

Then she thanked whatever power might still listen to her for blessing her with parents that passed on their flawless olive complexion. Amazingly, after riding through the Vegas night on the back of a motorcycle, being interrogated, and being fucked thoroughly and well by a man who could grace the cover of GQ, her face without makeup was not blotchy and would be the envy of every woman alive.

A little more snooping into the top drawers of his armoire rewarded her with big thick socks and black briefs that stayed up only after being rolled a few times. Seemed ridiculous after the man had literally explored every part of her body, but she didn't feel comfortable without something covering her girlie things.

Ready to storm the kitchen in her not-so-fashion-forward

outfit, she padded down the stairs. The fragrant aromas increased and by the time she reached the kitchen her stomach growled, then growled louder.

Her quick peek around in the daylight showed a large living room with a wall of windows that looked out onto a wraparound porch and a dense forest of trees. The furniture was rustic, like the bedroom with the same polished wood floors, and again she had to remind herself that this cozy mountain cabin was owned by an outlaw biker.

She entered the kitchen and stopped to admire the view. No, not the forest of majestic trees that surrounded the cabin. Her eyes fell on the hotter than hell man standing over the cooktop, shirtless, glorious tats in full view, sweats hanging dangerously low on his slim hips and bare feet. She didn't know if it would be considered a fetish, but she loved bare feet on a man. Then he looked up at her and smiled and damn if she didn't want to put her hunger on hold and drag him back to bed.

"You look hungry." The sexy rasp in his voice sounded like he'd spent the night fucking his brains out. Oh right, he had.

"Yes," she squeaked out, realizing he was waiting for an answer while she ogled him.

She moved closer to the griddle he'd laid across the burners. Pancakes, bacon and sausages on one side, with eggs frying on the other.

"And you said you couldn't cook," she teased.

"Breakfast, that's it." He smiled proudly. "Best meal of the day."

"So, the wine connoisseur is also a short order cook."

He waved the spatula over the griddle. "What would you like?"

"One of each."

"I'm impressed." He smiled. "I like a woman who eats."

She bit her tongue to keep her from bringing up Patrice, the last woman she'd seen cook him breakfast. Although it didn't look like she ate anything with that willowy figure.

"I know, you saw Patrice cooking me breakfast, but I never asked her to do that. That was just her trying to worm her way into my life."

Shit, how did he do that? How did he jump into her head like that? Creepy and bewildering at the same time.

"Right." She took the plate he offered her, then noticed he only scooped up the eggs for himself. Four eggs to be exact.

He nodded toward the slider. "Let's eat outside. Beautiful morning."

He was right, the clean mountain air held a bit of humidity, so refreshing after the dry desert air of Vegas. She breathed deep, enjoying the scent of flowers and foliage that surrounded the deck along with birds chirping in the distance.

They settled around a small round table and ate in comfortable silence.

She gazed at the pines swaying in the breeze, and let her mind drift to a life where living here with him would be a reality. Dangerous thoughts for a person who never planned past the next three days. Charting out a future never worked out for her. She thought she'd finish college, then her life fell apart and they shipped her to Vegas. Running scams hardly lends to long term planning, but now maybe—

Perfect. Too perfect.

HE COULD STARE at her face forever. Unbelievable the way she made his mind work. Thinking about the future. He never thought about the future. His or anyone else's. Except Danny, of course. He thought about his future all the time. How to keep all the special services he needed? How to make him as comfortable as possible? How to keep him a secret from his enemies?

That last one he fucked up good. Vinnie knew about him. The last person on earth he'd want sneaking around his brother, but he'd already notified Brookdale, then later today he'd look into moving him to another facility, cause there was no way he would take any more chances with his brother's wellbeing.

"What are you smiling at?" Cobra asked.

"The pine trees."

"Beautiful, right?"

Her face relaxed and her little sigh squeezed at his heart. He'd love to give her all this and more. Make her his. Yeah, his girl. Who knew for how long, but for right now, right here, she was all his and he was all hers.

"You're the first person who gets me. You're the only one I've confided in about my past." Her lips parted and her eyes widened like she hadn't meant to say that out loud.

"Don't hold back, I'm glad you said that."

"Doesn't matter anyway, you'd just read my mind like all the other times."

"You don't have to be a smart ass all the time, you know?"

"Defense mechanism." She shrugged. "Can't help it."

"My defense mechanism is pulling out my gun, so I guess making jokes is kinda harmless." He smiled. "We're good together. I could get used to this."

"You could never be with just one woman." She waved him off. "The first time some hot ass wiggled her way through the Gold Mine, you'd be on it."

His jaw clenched.

"Admit it, you could never be faithful."

Monogamy and him didn't go together for sure, but for her, hell yeah, maybe.

"You're right," he said. "But for you I'd try."

"Trying is not succeeding."

"Well, sometimes you just gotta have a little faith, babe."

She enveloped his hand in her small hands. "You're right."

He followed her gaze out into the cluster of pines towering over the cabin. Perfect time to tell her about Danny. Tell her the last piece of history about himself that could make or break their future. Explain how it all happened and then maybe even take her to meet Danny, if his whole story didn't turn her against him.

His phone buzzed in his pocket and he paused, but he didn't have the luxury of not answering his phone. Especially with Python on his ass about him neglecting the club.

He gave Sheena's hand a squeeze then glanced at the screen. His heart kicked up as he swiped the screen.

"Hello?"

"Mr. Dawson?"

Cobra swallowed hard. The last time Brookdale called in the middle of the day Danny had tried to get out of his wheelchair and fallen.

"Mr. Dawson, we've had to rush your brother to Sunrise Hospital. He was having trouble breathing and—"

"Fuck! Is he all right?" Cobra raked his hand through his hair.

"We don't know at this point. The ambulance took him ten minutes ago."

CHAPTER TWENTY-ONE

Fifteen minutes after Cobra raced off the porch Sheena realized how little she knew about him, or where she actually was. Yes, she knew she was on Mount Charleston, but that was a large area and she didn't even know the address, nor did she have any form of transportation to Vegas.

After he received the cryptic phone call, she followed him inside and listened to his incoherent mumblings about a brother and an emergency. She knew enough from Daisy that the MC members referred to each other as brother, so was he talking about one of them or an actual brother.

She'd told him to go and that she'd find a way home as Cobra threw on a t-shirt, his cut, laced up his boots, and flew out the door with a quick kiss and a promise to call her.

She'd called Daisy who volunteered to come get her and reassured her that as far as she knew nothing tragic had occurred inside the Serpents MC. Thanking whatever supreme being invented phone navigation she relayed the address etched onto the side of the mailbox at the end of Cobra's driveway.

"I don't know that much about Cobra." Daisy weaved her

car through the mountain roads. "Joker says he never mentions any family and is pretty closed off when it comes to that subject."

Sheena checked her phone for the hundredth time in sixty minutes. "He was totally undone. Frantic."

Now, after almost an hour Sheena hadn't heard from him and her street sense and disaster meter were on high alert.

———

COBRA PUSHED his bike to the limit, winding down the mountain roads and then exceeding the speed limit. When he finally pulled off Maryland Parkway and into the Sunrise Hospital parking lot, his back ached.

He stalked toward the Emergency Room entrance wishing he'd paid more attention to whoever called him from Brookdale, because he didn't have much information to go on. Except Danny was in trouble and at Sunrise.

He stormed the desk, well aware of the expression of the overworked clerk to his six-foot-three, unshaven, tatted body. Add that to the frenetic energy flying off him as he leaned over the counter and he was one scary mutherfucker.

"I'm looking for Daniel Dawson." The clerk tapped on the computer screen and Cobra added. "He was brought in about forty minutes ago from Brookdale Rehab."

She stopped tapping, but kept staring at the screen. Was this woman seriously trying to piss him off?

"You find him? Is he still in Emergency or did they get him a room?"

"No, he's—Are you a relative?"

"I'm his brother."

The woman stood, and pointed to some small cubicles lining the other side of the reception area. "If you would wait in Room 2 I'll have the doctor come in to speak to you."

"Is Danny still down here? Can I at least see him?"

"The doctor will be right with you, if you will just wait for him in Room 2."

Cobra sucked in some deep breaths. If he lost it on this woman he'd be hauled away, which would do neither him nor Danny any good. So he followed her direction and planted his ass in Room 2. The room measured eight feet square with two small upholstered chairs. Cobra didn't sit. He couldn't sit. He couldn't do anything until he saw Danny and found out what was wrong.

Twenty seconds, twenty minutes, Cobra didn't know exactly how long he'd been pacing that rectangular room. What he did know and what he'd never forget was the flat, expressionless manner of the doctor that entered, as he carefully closed the door behind him.

"Mr. Dawson, I'm sorry to inform you that your brother didn't make it." The doctor's voice devoid of emotion. "We tried to revive him, but unfortunately he was dead on arrival."

Cobra knew he opened his mouth, but the words didn't come. So many words he wanted to say, so many questions he wanted to ask, but nothing came.

"As I'm sure you know, your brother's health was compromised by his frail condition. We will be doing a toxicology report, and of course an autopsy, to determine the exact cause of death."

Cobra watched the doctor's mouth move, then he paused and waited, but Cobra remained mute. Unable to feel or respond.

"We have your brother's personal effects and if you'll wait here for just another minute, you can go in and see him."

Cobra sunk into the chair. Some time later a nurse led him

to another room at the end of the corridor. When Cobra hesitated, she turned the knob and he entered the horribly sterile, cold, barren room.

Danny lay on the stretcher covered to the neck with a sheet. His eyes closed, his body still. Cobra stared for a time, then moved closer. He laid his hand on Danny's shoulder. Still warm and for a split second Cobra thought maybe they'd made a mistake, but no. This was not a mistake, this was real.

"I'm sorry, buddy. Sorry for everything I didn't do and everything I did." Cobra kept his hand on Danny's shoulder relishing the last ounce of life that coursed through his brother.

Another unknown span of time passed and an orderly appeared. Cobra knew he couldn't stay there, but he hated leaving his baby brother with strangers. Hated how Danny had looked up to him, trusted him. Fine fuckin' job he did of protecting the only good thing in his miserable life.

Cobra leaned over and kissed his brother's forehead, then tousled his dark hair. "So, so sorry," he whispered in his ear.

———

COBRA LEFT the hospital and threw his leg over his bike, then squeezed the throttle and revved the engine one last time—For Danny. Maybe wherever he was, he'd heard it. Their last real connection. He didn't remember leaving the hospital or even the ride to his apartment.

He entered the penthouse at the same time his phone buzzed—Again. He yanked it out of his jeans pocket and glared at the ID. Python. He scrolled the rest of his missed calls and saw every member of the club and almost an even amount of messages and calls from Python and Sheena.

He stared at the list for longer than necessary. If he called any of them back what would he say. Yeah, I fucked up again. Put my selfish ass first again, and guess what, this time I killed my brother. A kid who never had a shot at life. A kid who was never able to be a kid. Raised by a vicious, crazy son of a bitch father who should've looked out for him, cared for him, loved him and instead . . .

Cobra's hands shook while his heart thudded in his chest. Hard pounding that he felt in his throat. He tried to suck in air, tried to regulate his breathing, but he lost the battle. His body was punishing him for all the shit he allowed to go down, all the missed opportunities. His body tortured him, knowing the damage he'd done, knowing how he'd failed the only person who needed him—The only person who loved him unconditionally.

The trembling of Cobra's hands spread to the rest of his body. The tremors made it difficult to stand. His head swam, the room whirled around him and he slapped his palm against the wall to steady himself seconds before a searing pain ripped through his gut.

Cobra wrapped his arms around his middle and crouched over hoping to ease the pain. Like a hot poker stabbing him over and over until—He raced to the kitchen and heaved into the sink. Emptying his stomach of all the hate, regret and sorrow. He braced his hands against the cool stainless steel and tried to breath.

He turned on the cold water, then splashed his face until his skin grew numb. He tried to regain his strength, tried to pull himself together, but it was no use. Nothing could ease this pain.

A CONSTANT TAPPING pulled Cobra away from the dark night sky. He ignored the irritating sound until it grew to a loud pounding. Fuckin' annoying. He sat for a few more seconds, and when he realized it was someone at the door he reluctantly pushed himself out of the chair and crunched over broken glass.

He flung the door open and came face to face with Python's glaring scowl.

"What the hell are you doin' and where the fuck you been?" Python pushed past Cobra, then stopped in the foyer. Hands balled in fists at his side. "I've been calling you, texting you."

Cobra walked back to the living room ignoring his questions.

"I thought you said you were gonna stop doin' your disappearing acts." Python dogged his steps. "You can't just go off without telling anybody. I told you to stop thinking with your dick, I told you to get your head on straight. That bitch is—"

Cobra spun around so fast Python stumbled backward catching himself on the edge of the couch.

"Get out," Cobra growled.

"What the fuck? I just got here. I've been trying to get ahold of you for twenty-four hours and now—"

"Get out," Cobra repeated.

Python crunched over the broken glass and stopped. "What the fuck happened?"

"I said, get out."

Python walked further into the penthouse and stopped. His gaze surveyed the turned over lamps, sofa and chair cushions thrown all over, and broken glass littering most of the tile and carpet. "Did somebody break in and trash the place?"

"Yeah, me." Cobra met Python toe to toe. "Now get the hell outta here."

"You did this?" Python rotated his head getting a good look. "What the hell?"

"I'm gonna tell you for the last time. Get. The. Fuck. Out." Cobra's voice raised with every word until it bounced off the walls.

Python examined him closely. "What's wrong with you, man?" His voice remained calm and low. The kind of voice you used on crazy people.

"Nothing. Just leave."

"I'm not going till you tell me what's going on with you."

Cobra reached behind him and pulled out his gun. He'd held the gun a few times over the last twenty-four hours debating on different ways to end this fucked up thing he called a life. The size and weight of it comforted him and now he pointed it at one of his brothers, his best friend since the beginning of the Serpents. The one man who knew him better than anyone—except maybe Sheena.

Python put his palms up but didn't move away from him. "C'mon, man dial it down. Tell me what's goin' on and we'll fix it."

"Can't fix this." Cobra waved the gun toward the door.

"Let's break open some of that high-end booze you got hidden away and get good and wasted," Python said over his shoulder as Cobra pushed him toward the door.

Cobra opened the door and shoved him through it. "Go."

Python eyeballed him and opened his mouth to say something seconds before Cobra slammed and locked the door.

Sheena flipped through endless cable TV channels and then just flipped the damn thing off. Wasn't doing anything to ease her nerves. Wasn't doing anything but making her madder.

195

She'd raised the ringer on her phone and included vibrate so there would be no way she would miss Cobra's call. When and if he called. Her concern very quickly escalated to terror and right about now she'd moved onto anger. Sheer unadulterated, ripping him a new one, anger.

The loud obnoxious sound of the Will and Grace theme song blared at her and she swiped up her phone and stared at the unknown number. Normally, she ignored these annoying sales calls, but who knew, maybe, just maybe it would have some connection to Cobra and where the hell he'd been for the last twelve hours.

"Hello?"

"What the fuck did you do to him?" A harsh, deep, very rude voice said.

"Excuse me? Who is this?"

"It's Python. Now tell me what the hell happened so I can get my boy right."

Her mouth fell open, then her lips clamped shut. How dare he automatically blame her for whatever was wrong.

"Hey, you still there?" He barked into the phone.

"Yes, I'm still here, and for your information I have no idea where Cobra is."

"Sure, you're innocent in all this. Like you haven't been fuckin' with his brain since that first night in the Gold Mine. Ya know, I tried to warn him about a bitch like you but—"

"Whoa," Sheena screamed into the phone and it felt good. She didn't know any more about Cobra, but the release was amazingly cathartic. "First of all, I haven't heard from him for twelve hours and secondly, how dare you lay all this shit on me."

"You haven't seen him?" His voice lowered slightly. Very slightly.

"That's what I just said you big ape. Something wrong

with your hearing?" She drew in a deep breath. That felt good too. "And furthermore, I'm worried about him too."

Now it was Python's turn to be silent.

"So why don't you rein it in, and tell me what you know so we can figure this out together."

Sheena heard the click of a lighter and the inhale of smoke. "I just left his apartment and he's all fucked up."

Her heart tripped off. "Fucked up, how? Physically? Was he in an accident?" Oh God, that would explain why he didn't call her. He was in traction, broken bones—

"No, nothing like that. He was out of mind. Trashed his place, but he wouldn't tell me what the hell was going on."

"When we were up at his cabin he got a phone call and he mumbled something about his brother."

"He took you to his cabin?"

Sheena pictured the shocked expression on Python's face.

"Yes. When he mentioned his brother, I thought he was talking about one of you guys."

"Nah, we're all good. Don't make sense. As far as I know he don't have any other family. Least none that he talks about."

"You said he was at his penthouse?"

"Yeah, looks like he's in some kind of a trance."

"I'm going over there." Sheena already had her shoes on and her purse in her hand. "I'll let you know how I make out."

"Thanks."

"You're welcome." She swiped at her phone and added. "You big jerk."

CHAPTER TWENTY-TWO

Cobra gazed out his window at the glittering lights of the Strip in the distance. When he'd first come to Vegas the people and excitement energized him. The last anxiety attack drained him and then the shit with Python. He had nothing left.

Over the years, he'd done some research online about anxiety. Most said to seek professional help to find your triggers, but he didn't need a shrink to figure that out. His triggers revolved around keeping Danny safe or anything related to how Danny got in that wheelchair in the first place. No mystery there. Only now Danny was gone.

Cobra blinked away the tears. He didn't deserve to cry. He'd hold onto this pain like a shield. The only memory of a broken life. Both his and Danny's.

He cocked his head at the familiar knocking. Goddamn Python back to butt into his business. He pushed himself out of the chair with more force than necessary. Maybe punching the annoying fuckers' face in would make him feel better. Yeah, that's what he would get for pissing him off.

"What part of leave me the fuck alone don't you under-stand?" Cobra flung the door open and froze.

Sheena.

His brain spun over the last twelve hours. Dragging her out of her apartment, taking her to the cabin, hot sex—Then the phone call that changed his life.

They stared at each other, then he turned from the door, and walked into the living room. She could go, she could stay, he didn't have the energy for another fight.

He heard the door close behind him and then her shoes crunching over the broken glass.

"Python called me."

He spit out a barking grunt. "Of course, he did. Miserable fucker just can't leave me alone, so he sent you."

"No, he didn't send me, I came on my own." She joined him in the living room. "I was worried about you."

"Funny, I'm worried about me too." He slumped into the chair.

"Let me help you fix whatever is wrong."

He threw back his head and laughed. Why did everybody think they could fix this, fix him. He laughed so hard it hurt and yet he couldn't stop until finally the bizarre laughter turned to sobbing. Gut heaving, twisting seizures of howling pain.

Sheena dropped down beside him and held him as his body shook and shivered. The harder he convulsed the harder she held him. Finally the sobbing subsided to choppy gasps.

"Take some deep breaths." Sheena stroked his hair.

He tried to push away from her but she wouldn't let him and he didn't have the strength to resist. He rested his head on her chest and concentrated on the beat of her heart.

"Please tell me what's wrong. Please tell me what has you so undone."

"I killed my brother."

SHE HELD HIM TIGHTER, happy he couldn't see her face or her shocked expression. Was he talking in riddles, or had he really killed someone?

After Sheena's phone call with Python, she had no idea what she'd be walking into. She decided against calling Cobra, reasoning that he probably wouldn't pick up, and a surprise visit would work best.

His insanely neat apartment was strewn with shards of glass, and turned over furniture. But that was nothing compared to the agony in Cobra's eyes. A pain so deep it hurt her to look at him, the way he broke apart, so fragile, so damaged.

She'd tried to hold him together, both physically and mentally, but she wasn't prepared for the words that spilled out.

"You're brother?" Again she wondered if he spoke of one of the Serpents.

"I should've protected him. Should've known what would happen. Vinnie doesn't make idle threats."

She didn't want to push him, but she needed more information. "Start at the beginning. Let me help you."

He drew in a deep cleansing breath and exhaled. "I have a brother—had a brother. Danny."

She stayed silent fearing any interruption would interrupt him.

"My life has been fucked up since the day I was born. My father called himself as survivalist. Fancy name for a nut job who dragged his family from one shit hole to the next, preaching the end of the world was coming. By the time we hit Nevada my father was crazier than ever. Seeing shit that wasn't real. Totally paranoid."

"What about your mother?"

He leaned over to the end table and retrieved a small framed picture. "Don't have much from my family, but people said I looked like her."

"Same eyes," Sheena said. "She was beautiful."

"A beautiful mess." Cobra sucked in a deep breath. "My father had her strung out on heroin, which was how he controlled her. By sixteen I'd had enough of my father's bullshit. I tried to defend my mother, but that didn't end well. She sided with him and I ended up out in the desert."

Sheena furrowed her brow.

"Sierra Home for Boys. A shit hole where they send kids nobody wants. No locks, no gates. You could walk out anytime you wanted if you didn't mind spending days in the desert with no food or water."

"That's terrible."

"Some guys tried. They'd find the dead bodies a few days later. Snake bites, heat stroke."

"How did they get away with that?"

"Did you miss the part where I said we were sent there because nobody cared. These people didn't give a shit about us as long as they were getting paid from the government. Half the time we only got one meal a day because the supervisors were pocketing the money."

"Oh my god."

"After six months I couldn't take it anymore, so I left. I can remember the guard laughing, telling me they'd have one less mouth to feed."

"Weren't you scared?"

"I didn't care if I died." Cobra closed his eyes for a second. "Some parts are a blur. The heat was brutal. I finally collapsed under this low scrub. I must've passed out and when I woke up a rattler was coiled inches from my foot. He stared at me and I figured I was done. He reared up and I braced myself, but he turned and slithered away. Either the snake didn't feel I was worth the effort or I was given a second chance. I went with the second chance theory."

"Las Vegas Serpents."

"A few years later I got into a bar fight with a biker. After we shed some blood, I found out that most of his brothers were caught in a DEA sting and there was nothing left of his club. We ended up getting stinking drunk, and when we sobered up we combined our skills, and the Serpents were born. The biker was Python."

"I'm completely blown away." She swiped at the tear. "I can't believe all you've been through."

A harrowing story, but no mention of a brother. She stayed silent willing him to continue, yet not sure if she wanted to hear more heartbreak.

"By then my mother had another baby. Another boy—Danny. Probably because of all the junk in my mother's body, he was small and had some health issues. He was six when they sent me away, I'd go back over the years to visit him, but I had nothing to offer the kid. Then when we got the Serpents together, I finally had some money saved. He was about eleven and he was so excited, so happy that he could finally leave that rathole of a trailer. My father went to his survivalist meetings every Saturday morning, so the plan was to get Danny and take him to the clubhouse. To safety."

Cobra shifted and scrubbed his hand over his face and Sheena braced for the worst.

"That Friday night we had a big party at our old clubhouse celebrating the one-year anniversary of the Serpents. Biker parties go on for hours, sometimes days. I got so wasted that I didn't wake up till Sunday morning. One day late."

Sheena's stomach knotted up.

"I drove out to the trailer and there was Danny crumbled up on the kitchen floor, blood all over, alone." Cobra squeezed his eyes shut. "The paramedics said it was a miracle he was alive, but the damage to his spinal cord and his brain couldn't be repaired."

"I'm so sorry, baby."

"He's spent the rest of his days strapped in a wheelchair with limited speech and the mentality of an eleven-year-old. Like his brain stood still."

"Your father did it?"

"My father hated Danny 'cause he was small and fragile. Not survivalist material. I knew he was hitting the kid, that's why I wanted to get him out of there."

"You tried."

"Tried and fuckin' failed," he yelled. "I was partying and screwing every pussy in the clubhouse while my little brother was getting his brains beat in—Literally."

"No, you can't blame yourself for that."

"Well you're a little late, babe, 'cause I've been blaming myself for the last ten years." Cobra dropped his head to his hands. "And now he's dead."

"Danny died?" Sheena's heart stuttered.

"That was the call I got this morning."

She wrapped him in her arms willing the pain to leave him. "I'm so sorry." They stayed like that for a few minutes and then she pulled back. "Was it because of his other health issues?"

When he raised his head, his eyes were focused and clear. "No, Vinnie murdered him."

"You know this?" Her eyes widened, but she couldn't

process what he was saying.

"After Danny got hurt money was tight. He needed treatments and Vinnie needed a partner and an inside guy to run the weed farms and other shit. Vinnie gave me the money I needed for Danny and to buy the Gold Mine and I gave him the man power."

Cobra shifted and dragged in a ragged breath.

"When I found Ecstasy it was a rundown joint always getting raided. I had some good ideas, brought the investment to Vinnie and he liked it."

"You became partners."

"By the time the lease was signed on Ecstasy I'd already made my deal with the devil."

"So, he knew about Danny."

"No. Nobody knew about my brother. Not even Python. I felt the only way to keep Danny truly safe was to keep him far away from my life."

"So, what makes you think—"

"Cause when I tried to cut him out of our deal he threatened Danny. It blew me away that he knew about him, but he probably had me followed or some shit. He's got eyes all over. I should've been more careful, I should've—"

"No, don't do that. Don't blame yourself."

"Who the fuck else can I blame?" Cobra raked his hands through his hair. "Danny was my responsibility and I failed him twice. The first time put him in a wheelchair and the second time killed him."

"Do you have any proof that it was Vinnie? I mean if Danny was in an institution how would he get to him?"

"Vinnie's a cold-blooded bastard who would do anything to get his own way. That's my proof."

CHAPTER TWENTY-THREE

Sheena snuggled in next to him on the oversized chair and cradled his head to her chest. "I can't imagine your pain, but I do know that guilt is a terrible thing to carry around. It's a burden that only gets heavier."

He lifted his head and stared into her eyes. This close, he could see the depth of her ebony eyes along with a warmth he wished he could give her in return. She ran her hand through his hair and then lightly massaged his shoulder. The tightness relaxed as her hands worked their magic.

She shifted and drew him to her again, placing little butterfly kisses against his neck. Soothing him with her soft touch. Nurturing him with an affection he'd never known. For the first time in his miserable life he felt cared for, and that maybe for a little while he could lay down his sword and surrender. Resign himself to being human.

He pushed her beautiful hair away, and cupped her face in his hands. "I need you."

Without a word she stood pulling him with her. They crunched over his mess and sidestepped around random furniture cushions as she led him into the bedroom.

She sat next to him on the bed making gentle circles over his shoulders. Her touch burned through his t-shirt, relaxing his muscles.

All the other times they'd been together it was a frantic race to clash together, to release the tension, but this time was different. They came together as two broken souls, both searching, both seeking something tangible to hold onto.

She lifted his t-shirt up and over his head, then gently pushed him against the mattress. He laced his fingers behind his head and she stilled.

"I think this is a very good time for you to finally tell me about the meaning of Sacrifice and Redemption."

His first instinct was to shut her down. Not get into the deep emotions that made him mark his skin, but what did it matter now. She'd seen him at his lowest, she knew all his secrets, so she might as well know this as well.

"Sacrifice I got on my thirtieth birthday. The word holds so many different meanings for me, but mainly it's what I've done for most of my life. Sometimes the sacrifice was too large, but somehow I survived. I guess you could say it's about survival and reminding me that no sacrifice is too much."

"I'm sure you sacrificed a lot for Danny."

"He was never a sacrifice." He stared at the ceiling. "He was just a sweet innocent kid who never had a chance."

"And Redemption?"

"That one has two meanings for me. Before we got the Serpents together, I was basically blowing my life apart 'cause I had no direction. Nothing to believe in. I ended up doing a stint in Ely and after I was released and done with probation, I wanted to declare my freedom. I also hoped by inking it on my skin that I would find some peace regarding what happened to Danny, but that theory never worked. The guilt never subsided."

"Two such powerful words, and the meaning you've put behind them is impressive."

He pulled her onto him and she straddled his waist. "You're the only one who knows their true meaning. The only one I ever wanted to share it with."

"You know I understand how guilt and regret feel." She leaned in and gently kissed him.

He wrapped his arms around her and held her tight to him, loving the warmth of her body. They kissed and nipped at each other for longer than usual. Each sensing the need to relish the moment and take it slower. The last few days were tough. Cobra needed closure. He needed to settle the score with Vinnie.

Sheena worked him through his sweats, then snaked her hand under his waistband. As with every time before, his cock came to life and all his brain could process was making her his.

She leaned away from him and removed her jeans. He tried to help, but she pushed him away letting him know that this was her show. It felt good to let go and not be in charge for once.

He lifted his hips and she pulled at his sweats, then flung them behind her, and crawled up his body like a panther on the prowl. All wild hair, sleek body and golden skin. He ran his hands over her hips and cupped her ass.

Her slow, deliberate rocking made his eyes cross, but neither of them wanted to rush. She reached for his bedside table, pulled out a condom, placed it between her perfect white teeth and ripped it open. Her delicate fingers slowly slide it on, and he bit back a growl. He needed to be in her and in her now. She positioned herself over him again, and after a few teasing thrusts, she finally let him slide in.

Cupping her neck, he pulled her down to his waiting lips. He needed to connect, to meld and move together with their mouths joined in rhythm with their bodies. Perfect and absolute, like nothing else mattered around them. Safe in their protected cocoon for just a little while.

When he gripped her ass, she broke away from his lips and they rocked in perfect unison, her hands braced on his chest. Gliding and sliding over him. He watched, loving how her body took him in. The sight of it almost made him blow apart.

He nipped at her shoulder, then rubbed his stubbled chin against the bite until she trembled. The quiver of her body amped him up even more. He trailed his lips down the slim column of her neck until he reached the rise of her breasts.

"Love this," he growled into her soft flesh. Then captured her nipple between his lips and drew on it until she moaned out. "And I love the sounds you make when I suck on them. Fuckin' crazy hot."

He switched to the other side and her fingers dug into his hair, keeping him exactly where he wanted to be. He could spend the rest of his life exploring her body and it still wouldn't be enough. He'd still need more, but for once in his selfish life he knew what he had to do. It would wreck him, but he would do it, because a woman like Sheena deserved so much more, so much better.

The harder he sucked on her nipple the faster she moved over him. Their bodies slapped together in an uncontrollable frenzy. Trapped between a need to find his shattering release and the dread of it all coming to an end. He held onto her tight, wanting to remember every plane of her body. The way it curved and dipped, then putting her scent to memory.

"I promise to do right by you," he gasped out, hoping she would understand his decision.

She stilled for a second, then her pants turned to groans and he knew she was close. When he felt the blistering heat of her body release and squeeze him he gave in to the sensations that consumed him.

"Fuck!" he shouted out, then let go, following close behind her, reveling in the aftershocks of her perfect body. They laid still, him caressing the soft skin of her back, and thinking he'd be adding another meaning to his Sacrifice tattoo.

"That was unbelievable . . . in so many ways. We were so in sync, so together," she gasped.

"Mmmm." He brushed her hair aside and nibbled on her neck as he searched for the best way to let her go. Impossible. There was no easy way. He wanted to say so much to her. Thank her for being here for him, but anything now would sound fake especially since he had to turn her away.

Cobra stared at the gorgeous woman above him. The black depths of her eyes, the way her body moved under him, above him. It didn't matter as long as she was near him, but now all that had to be over.

He could just hear Python calling him a pussy, telling him to get over himself, but what he felt with Sheena went way beyond fucking her bangin' body. If this thing they had wasn't so different he wouldn't be forced to act so drastically.

"I guess you've figured out we can't stay like this forever."

She cocked her head obviously confused by his words. "Here in your room?"

"No, me and you. I tried to fool myself, but I can't give you what you want."

"We haven't even discussed what we want, so—"

Just spit it the fuck out and don't be a pussy.

"You don't get it, babe. I got nothing to give. I'm empty inside."

He had to give up the only good thing left in his life. He had to set her free while she still had a chance because a life with him was not possible.

"Empty? What the hell is that supposed to mean?"

He'd never subject someone he cared so much about to his mess.

"You should have a guy who can express his feelings. A guy who will take care of you and understand your feelings." He raked his hand through his hair. "That's not me."

"That's not true. You've already showed me so many emotions."

He pounded on his chest. "Nothing in there but anger."

No, as sweet as this was and as much as she'd given him. It ended now.

She sat up, letting the sheet fall away from her body. "I won't let you sell yourself short."

He jackknifed off the bed. "You've seen what happens to me. The shit storm that goes through my body. I'm damaged."

"Because you get some panic attacks? I can handle that."

"But you shouldn't have to. Don't you get it. You deserve the best, and I ain't it."

He'd greedily taken her body, but let him do one unselfish act in setting her free of him and all his baggage. He had no idea how he'd go on, but there were some dangerous shit he had to take care of, and he wasn't about to let her get caught in the crossfire again.

"It'll be easier if you just go." He pulled on his sweatpants.

"Easier for who?"

"Both of us."

She opened her mouth, but nothing came. He'd broken the sass right out of her. It tore him up to watch her hold in the tears, watch her put up that thick coat of armor he'd stripped away, but he knew he was doing the right thing.

She silently dressed, and he left the room. He couldn't look at her face, couldn't bear to see her pain, 'cause right now his own pain sucked the life out of him.

After she left, he pulled out his phone. The arrogant prick answered on the second ring. "I wondered how long it would take for you to call me."

"No games, I'm done," Cobra barked into the phone.

"You don't know how happy I am to hear that."

"Just own what you did." Cobra pounded his fist against the living room wall. "Admit that you killed my brother."

"Why don't you come to Ecstasy where we can talk in private."

"Fuck that, you want private, meet me in the tunnels," Cobra said.

Vinnie went silent. The Vegas storm drains were legend and a home to every druggy, thief and degenerate in the city. Miles of tunnels that ran under the Strip were supposed to drain flood water, but became a sketchy underground world for the forgotten. The entrance to one of them was right behind Ecstasy.

"Fine," Vinnie finally said. "I'll meet you there at midnight."

"Midnight." Cobra repeated. "Just you and me. No tricks."

Cobra swiped his phone, then grabbed up his gun on the coffee table. He weighed the heavy weapon in his hand. It gave him purpose and a feeling of closure. Him and Vinnie, head to head. No interference, no bullshit. The goal was to make Vinnie pay, but Cobra didn't care if he walked away or not. He would accept however the night ended.

"I THOUGHT I told you to call the minute you got there," Python barked into the phone.

"And as I told you. I don't take orders from you." Sheena heard the click of Python's lighter and a long exhale.

"Cobra might like your sass. Might even turn him on, but it does shit for me so let's get down to it. How is he?"

She pushed down the pain of Cobra's rejection because she knew it came from a place of pain. His way of protecting her, and now putting up with Python and giving him all the information was her way of protecting him.

"You were right, he was struggling big time," Sheena said. Even a dog needed a bone once in a while. "Then he told me his brother Danny died."

Silence again, then. "I didn't know he had a brother."

"Apparently, no one did. Danny was in a wheelchair living at Brookdale Rehabilitation. Cobra blames himself for what put Danny in the wheelchair and for his death."

She didn't feel comfortable relaying the whole story, since it wasn't her story to tell.

"No wonder he went off the rails."

"And . . . He thinks Vinnie's responsible for Danny's death."

"Shit. That is fucked up."

"He shut down and made me leave, but there is something else."

"Spill."

"I heard him on the phone and I'm almost positive he was talking to Vinnie about meeting with him at midnight."

"I thought you said he made you leave."

"Did you forget that I'm a con artist first and always? As I left, I blocked the door with the deadbolt and snuck back in."

"Sweet."

Finally, a compliment from the big jerk.

"I only heard his side of the conversation, but I think he said, in the tunnels?"

"Makes sense."

"Where's the tunnels?"

"Behind Ecstasy."

"You mean the storm drains?"

"We use them for our more private meetings."

The tone of Python's voice was enough to tell her not to ask any more questions.

"He sounded so desperate. It was a mix of defeat and anguish. I was thinking—"

"Stop right there. There is no fuckin' way you're going anywhere near this."

"I just thought that—"

"Forget it. Unless you're gonna tell me that you're bringing four guys bigger than me for back up, I'm not interested. I'll be there and I'll make sure he's safe."

Python pissed her off big time, but she didn't want to see either of them involved in a murder. His own or anyone else's, and if anything happened to Cobra—

"Instead of being a Neanderthal you could at least listen to me. I think when I tell you who I am, and who I know you'll change your mind."

Time to take matters into her own hands.

CHAPTER TWENTY-FOUR

"You didn't actually think Python would be up with your idea, did you?" Daisy said as she drove down Flamingo on their way to Ecstasy.

"I expected him to listen, not to just dismiss me like I'm some naive little girl." Sheena drummed her fingers against her thigh, but it did nothing to relieve the tension that coursed through her body.

"That's the MC mentality. Joker is a constant work in progress, but so worth it."

The lilt of love in Daisy's voice tugged at Sheena's heart. She'd hoped for that with Cobra, and was determined to help him even if he didn't think he needed it.

"Spoken like a true newlywed."

"Python is truly worried about Cobra," Daisy said. "According to Joker their bond is as strong as blood brothers. Maybe stronger now that Cobra lost his real brother."

"It's just so frustrating. Even after I told Python my background he only half listened, then only agreed with me because I told him I wouldn't stay away. As if?" Sheena gazed out the passenger side window. "No way I'm letting this go down without my help. Especially when I feel partly responsible."

"No way you're responsible," Daisy countered.

"I've been in Vegas working for Vinnie and Cobra's been in Vegas using Vinnie as a silent partner. Then Cobra and I get together and Vinnie isn't so silent anymore. I don't believe in coincidences."

They stopped at a light and Daisy turned to Sheena. "Just please be careful. We both know Vinnie plays for real and from what you've told me he's acting desperate."

"We've dealt with desperate before." Sheena shot Daisy a knowing look.

"True, but desperate and crazy can be a deadly combination."

Sheena appreciated Daisy's concern, but Cobra's ability to think rationally died with Danny. Now, it was up to her to save him from himself and Vinnie's irrational wrath.

"COMING DOWN HERE WITHOUT ANY BACKUP?" Joker said, as him and Python picked their way down the cracked cement that led to the mouth of the drainage tunnel behind Ecstasy. "What the hell did he think was gonna happen?"

"That's the problem, he's not thinking," Python said.

"I still can't believe he had a brother, and that Vinnie killed him. That's fucked up."

"And now it's up to us to un-fuck it." They positioned themselves off to the side of the cement tunnel behind some scrubby bushes. "Me and Cobra started the Serpents. He's a good president. Always fair, but this shit with Vinnie just got way outta hand, and the more Cobra tried to shut him down the crazier Vinnie got. The fucker just couldn't stand that we didn't need him anymore."

"I get working for crazy," Joker said.

Python remembered Joker's psycho president from their East Coast chapter. "Also didn't help that Cobra got twisted up with Sheena at the same time we were looking to make a break."

"I've only known Sheena for a few months, but if she's Daisy's friend she's all right," Joker said.

Python trusted Joker's opinion, but sometimes Sheena was a little too mouthy for his taste. Sure she was hot as fuck, but Python liked his women quiet and bitch-free."

Joker turned toward the cavernous tunnels. "What is this place?"

"Supposed to catch the excess water and keep the city from flooding, but it's turned into home for every skell in Vegas."

Joker walked in a few feet and then back out. "Shit, it stinks."

"Sucks how some people have to live." Python jerked his chin toward the tweakers hovering just inside the entrance. "I bring them food sometimes from Ecstasy."

Joker did a double take. "Who knew? The MC enforcer is a humanitarian."

"Don't spread it around." Python smirked. "Gotta keep up my rep."

Joker laughed without humor as his eyes roamed over the filthy clothes and dirty faces of two of the guys huddled together. "I know a little bit about being desperate and falling between the cracks, but this is a whole other level of fucked."

Python clapped Joker's shoulder. "Thanks for stepping up tonight. Didn't wanna pull any of the Serpents in on this incase we're being watched. One thing we sure don't want Metro in on."

THE UNDERGROUND DRAINAGE tunnels were only five hundred feet behind the lot of Ecstasy, but they might as well be five hundred miles. Cobra knew he could be walking into a trap, but for some insane reason he needed to hear Vinnie admit that he killed Danny. His own fucked up version of closure. Plus, he had nothing else to lose. Danny was gone and he'd already given up Sheena. He shoved her away because he couldn't have any distractions when it came to this final showdown.

He left the smooth blacktop of Ecstasy's parking lot and tramped over the loose rock and broken concrete path that led to the entrance of the tunnels. Shadows from Ecstasy's security lights flickered over the area. The hairs on the back of his neck tingled as the stink of sewage and despair surrounded him. A perfect place to meet the psycho who sent his life straight to hell.

"It pains me that things had to end up this way." Vinnie stepped out of the murky darkness.

Cobra's fists balled and his first instinct was to reach for his gun. Make it fast and easy, but his gut wouldn't let him. His gut and his heart needed to hear the words that broke him in two.

"You just wouldn't stop pushing," Cobra accused. "You had to have it all."

Vinnie waggled his finger like a parent scolding a toddler. "I think it was you and your band of thugs that got greedy."

"Cut the bullshit and admit it. You killed my brother."

Cobra braced himself for the truth. Knowing it would rip him apart all over again.

"I warned you what would happen if you didn't pay up." Vinnie blew out a long dramatic sigh.

Cobra's mind spun in all directions. He couldn't handle anymore mind games or tricks.

"Just say it," Cobra demanded.

"Yes, I killed him." Vinnie shrugged. "Because you ignoring me wasn't smart."

"How?" The pain coursed through him like hot lava, but he had to know. "I restricted all visitors."

"You can't believe that would've kept me out." Vinnie tilted his head in an annoying fucking way. "I merely flashed my fake credentials, and told them I was a new doctor you sent to examine Danny."

Vinnie's words ricocheted around Cobra's brain. "Don't say his name."

"I gave you every opportunity to make things right. So, in a way his death makes you just as guilty."

Cobra mentally accused himself of the same crime. Tortured himself with panic and anxiety, but hearing it out of Vinnie's mouth sent Cobra over the edge.

"You are the worst kinda fuckin' animal," Cobra growled.

DAISY PARKED the car in Ecstasy's lot, then moved to the edge of the blacktop and stopped. At the bottom of the ridge, Vinnie and Cobra faced each other. Too far away to hear the conversation, but Cobra's body language explained it all.

Sheena cut her eyes to Daisy. "You ready to do this?"

"It's showtime."

They moved down the embankment, making as much

noise as possible while Sheena concentrated on playing her best, most dangerous con ever.

"I keep telling you this is a bad idea," Daisy shouted at Sheena.

"And I keep telling you to mind your own business," Sheena shot back attitude dripping off of every word.

"RIGHT ON SCHEDULE." Python checked his gun then shoved it into his waistband.

"Let's get this done." Joker and Python did a fist bump.

"What the hell is wrong with you," Python bellowed, as he came into sight. "I thought I told you to stay the fuck away from here."

"Yeah, and dragging my wife into your shit is not cool." Joker flanked Python on the other side.

"What the hell is going on?" Vinnie's head swung toward Sheena and Daisy, and then Python and Cobra as a split second of confusion covered his face.

"I want to settle my shit with you once and for all," Sheena stepped to Vinnie. "You had no right telling him," she jerked her thumb at Cobra, "about my past and my real name."

"We were having a private conversation here," Vinnie barely kept the menace out of his strained voice as he motioned to Cobra.

"It would've been nice if you kept my life story private too," Sheena said, with all her Jersey attitude. "Cause now you scared him off and he threw me the hell out and I'm pissed. So sorry, not sorry."

Cobra's fists flexed at his side. The sight of Sheena and Daisy coming toward them had his heart beating in his throat. Then Python and Joker popping up out of nowhere. What the ever-loving fuck was going on?

"Hey babe, we ain't interested in your sad love life. My brother here can get all the pussy he wants, whenever he wants it." Python slung his arm around Cobra's shoulders and when Vinnie's gaze darted to Sheena, Python used the opportunity to lean into Cobra. "Play along," he whispered, then said out loud, "Ain't that right, brother."

"Hell yeah," Cobra answered without hesitation. "But I bet the boys back East wouldn't like you pissing off the mob princess."

Cobra saw how this would work. He'd draw the attention on him and give Python and Joker enough room to move in. Great fuckin' idea if he could take Sheena out of the equation.

"How about I give them a call." Sheena flipped out her phone. "And we'll see how they feel about you giving away all my secrets. Which are actually their secrets too."

"Your trust was my insurance." Vinnie whipped out his gun. "So nobody's making any phone calls."

Cobra's head swam at the sight of a gun pointed at Sheena. "Put the phone down, babe," Cobra warned.

Python said to play along, but Sheena purposely goading a vicious scumbag like Vinnie couldn't be part of the plan. Vinnie didn't care that she was a woman or without a weapon, he only cared about survival.

He tried to catch her line of vision, but she'd zeroed in on Vinnie, determined to push him to the edge.

"Too late, I'm tired of being a puppet. I'm tired of dancing to his tune." Sheena held the phone out taunting Vinnie, then hit the screen and put the phone to her ear. "I think they'd like to know how you wasted all that money they sent you to keep my identity quiet, and how you made it personal to settle your grudge with Cobra."

"I warned you, bitch." Vinnie raised the gun, pointed it at Sheena's chest and pulled the trigger a second before Cobra lunged. Sheena fell to the ground, and another shot rang out behind them. Vinnie dropped the gun then held his bloody hand to his chest.

Cobra dropped next to Sheena shielding her with his body, "Shit baby, stay still."

The two tweakers Cobra saw lounging by the entrance of the tunnel charged toward them with guns drawn. The bald one grabbed Vinnie in a tight hold from behind while the other tweaker held him at gunpoint.

"Who the fuck are you?" Vinnie spit out.

"Wasn't smart thinking you could steal from your friends in Jersey. Thinking you were smarter than us." The guy waved his gun in Vinnie's face.

"I don't know what you're talking about," Vinnie blustered.

"The money you're supposed to send us every month, fucker." Baldy pulled Vinnie tighter. "You pissed it away and then tried to drag us into human trafficking just to cover your ass. Not smart."

Cobra hovered over Sheena as her blood seeped into the dirt. "It's gonna be okay. Just stay with me."

Cobra pushed down the instinct to pull his own piece knowing any sudden movement might spook the guy, and put Sheena in more danger. Her eyes flicked to his like she wanted to tell him something, but Vinnie's voice drew Cobra to the drama playing out above them.

"They're filling your head with lies." Vinnie jerked his head at Cobra and Python.

"And who do you think the boys back East will believe?"

Baldy said. "The fucker who's been stealing from them or the witnesses who have nothing to gain?"

"All right," Vinnie said. "What do you want?"

"We'd like our money, but since everybody's lost their patience we'll settle for making you an example."

Cobra's gaze focused on Sheena as Joker and Python stood to the side, and let Vinnie finally get what he deserved.

Vinnie's eyes widened at the realization. "An example?" Vinnie squeaked out.

"They gave you a job to do and sent you out here to make money, and you fucked that up by skimming from them. Then they sent her out here under your protection and you go and fuckin' shoot her. Not gonna sit well."

"Let's try to figure this out," Vinnie reasoned. "You want me to disappear I'll change my zip code. Hell, I'll change my fucking country code."

Cobra cradled Sheena to him as Vinnie tried to wheedle his way out of a no-win situation. "Just hang in there, baby."

Shoot the fucker so I can get my girl outta here. He couldn't deny it. No matter what, she'd always be his girl.

"I'm getting tired of listening to him. How about you?" The guy holding Vinnie nodded, then threw him to the ground.

"Time's up fucker." Two quick pops. One in the balls and one between his eyes. Vinnie's body jerked once, then lay still.

Revenge for Danny's death was sweet, but it didn't bring him back. Only time would heal the pit of remorse that coursed through him. His only regret was that he hadn't pulled the trigger himself.

The shooter toed Vinnie's lifeless corpse until it rolled down the slight incline landing at the mouth of the tunnels.

The determined expressions plastered across their stone faces told Cobra they were professionals.

Cobra stroked the hair away from Sheena's face. "Everything's gonna be okay. You're gonna be all right."

She had to be because there was no way Cobra could survive losing someone else he—Loved?

CHAPTER TWENTY-FIVE

Python poured himself and Cobra another shot. "The longer you sit here drumming your fingers against the table the more time you're wasting."

After the shootout, Cobra closed the Gold Mine down to recoup and make sense out of what happened. Seemed like he was the only one cut out of the loop and it pissed him the fuck off.

"I just can't believe she'd do something so stupid." Cobra slammed his fist against the table so hard Python's beer bottle toppled over. "Fuckin' ridiculous."

"I wasn't up with Sheena's plan at first either, but you gotta admit, it worked," Python said.

"And that's another thing." Cobra pointed his finger at Python. "You let her go through with it, and you didn't say shit about it to me."

"Look, she can be mouthy, but she's also ballsy and keeping you out of it was the only way to make it work." Python cocked his eyebrow. "Although you calling her out afterwards and losing your shit probably wasn't the way to go."

"And don't go telling me I handled her all wrong, 'cause I already know that." Cobra stuck a cigarette between his teeth.

"You sure did." Daisy slammed the door behind her. The sound echoing in the empty bar as she stalked to their table.

Cobra scrubbed his hand over his scruffy jaw. "How pissed is she?"

"Well, let's see. She came up with a brilliant plan, played Vinnie perfectly and then you act like an ungrateful ass."

"She offered herself up for bait. Aside from the fact that I nearly had a fuckin' heart attack, and a million things could've gone wrong, it was all good."

"But a million things didn't go wrong, and it all went down as she planned." Daisy slammed her hands on her hips. "The only thing you didn't like was not being in charge."

"Hate to say it fucker, but she's right," Python slugged some beer.

"You're just pissed 'cause you were left outta the loop," Joker added. "Same shit happened to me when Daisy and I were in Miami."

Cobra flipped them off, hating that they were right. "Says the pussy-whipped newlywed."

"But I won't be sleeping alone tonight." Joker wrapped his arm around Daisy's waist. "I gotta say these women are fearless."

"A little too fearless." Cobra sucked on his cigarette. "When I think of what could've—Shit!" He slammed his fist on the table again, and Python grabbed up his beer to keep it from spilling again.

"She's not very happy with you right now," Daisy said.

"I don't care if she's happy, she scared the shit outta me."

"We'll see who's happy later when your ass is lying alone in that big bed of yours." Joker laughed.

Daisy pulled up a chair. "So, how're you going to make this right?"

Cobra dragged deep on his cigarette, and blew the smoke toward the ceiling. "You're the one with all the answers, you tell me."

SHEENA PACED her small living room because she couldn't sit still. After Daisy dropped her off, her emotions spun in all directions. From relief and pride of a job well done, to uncontrollable fury at Cobra's chauvinist, outdated beliefs regarding women.

His lack of faith in her and what she tried to do infuriated her to the point of violence. The only reason she didn't throw something across the room right now was because she knew, in the end, she'd have to clean it up. Not much satisfaction there.

The knocking on the door startled her out of her fit of frustration. Then the knocking turned to pounding, along with yelling. "Open the damn door, Sheena. I know you're in there."

"Go away," she yelled through the dead-bolted and chain locked door.

"I ain't leaving, so unless you want your neighbors hearing your business I suggest you open this door."

"Fine, let everyone know what a small-minded misogynist you are."

"A what?"

"Would it've been so hard to say thank you, to say that I did a good job and that my plan was brilliant?"

"I'm not gonna keep screaming through this damn door. So you better . . ."

She unlocked the door and peeked through the opening with the security chain still in place. She'd installed the chain after his last break-in, but his big, booted feet made the flimsy lock seem ridiculous.

"You realize that in two seconds I could boot this door, right?"

Yup, once again they were thinking the same thing. Creepy. She sucked in a deep breath. Her downstairs neighbor was already banging on the ceiling and the last thing either one of them needed was the police sniffing around, so she undid the chain and opened the door.

He moved into her small living room, she closed the door, and they silently stared at each other. He looked worn out and weary. His hair stood on end like he'd been dragging a rake through it and his beautiful blue eyes were hooded and heavy with exhaustion. He held his body in a rigid, tight way that screamed pent up tension.

"What the hell were you thinking?" Cobra roared.

"I was thinking that I did a damn good job setting Vinnie up."

"By offering yourself up as a human target?" He pushed his fingers through his tangled hair. "Fuck Sheena, when Vinnie shot you I almost lost my shit."

"I knew what I was doing." She motioned to the front of her shirt. She'd been in such a fury when she got home she didn't even change. "Bullet proof vest and a fake blood packet. Works every time."

"I know you've done some crazy shit before, but getting someone to draw on you?"

Sheena didn't feel the need to answer him. Yes, they'd done variations of the fake shooting, but that wasn't the point. "The bottom line is, it worked."

"And the shooters?"

"I still have one or two people I can count on in Jersey. They were already disgusted with Vinnie and the way he was handling things here. Apparently, they'd been watching him for months, so all they needed was a little push. Mission accomplished."

In three large steps he closed the distance between them and slapped his hands against the door on each side of her head.

"Fuckin' crazy." Cobra dropped his head into her neck and growled. "You ever put yourself out there like that again and—"

"You didn't mind when I ran that con for Joker out in the desert last month, so I don't understand all the drama now."

His heavy sigh warmed the base of her neck. "Cause last month we weren't us and you weren't mine. Don't you get it, if anything ever happened to you I'd—" His voice choked and she stroked the side of his face.

"If you're in trouble, I would do the same thing all over again, so don't even bother warning me." She dug her fingers into his unruly hair and tugged. "I won't stand behind you, I'll stand alongside you. Always."

He bit the skin of her collarbone and she yelped. He nibbled his way up to the lobe of her ear and the tiny little nips made her stomach flutter.

"When Danny died I crashed." He stared into her eyes, only inches apart. "If it wasn't for you I . . . I can't lose you."

The pain and anguish in his voice broke her. She wrapped her arms around his shoulders and his palms skated down her back, pulling her closer.

"You won't," she whispered into his ear. "Ever."

They stood like that for a few long minutes. Her holding him close, him holding her closer. The emotion in his voice was deep. A pain from long ago, a pain that laid on the surface and threatened to implode. She guessed his panic attacks were a result of this trauma, and she silently vowed to work with him to conquer them and rid him of the demons that tortured him.

He unwound his arms and took a half step back. "Take that shit off. Even though I know it's fake blood it creeps me the fuck out." His fingers fumbled with the buttons of her shirt.

She pushed his hand away and undid the rest exposing the Kevlar vest.

"Un-fuckin-believable."

He helped her undo the Velcro straps, pulled it over her head and stopped. He stared at the bruising just above her heart from the impact of the bullet.

"Shit, babe." He ran his fingertips over the mark. "That tears me up."

"It's nothing. A small price to pay."

He cupped her breasts with both hands, lowered his lips to her nipple and she sighed out, holding his head in place.

"Need to fuck you, babe," he mumbled against her flesh. "Need to show you how much you mean to me. How much I want you."

He scooped her up and headed for her bedroom.

"The first time you carried me like this I was drunk on tequila." She traced her finger over the tat on the underside of his forearm. "The first time I saw these great tats."

"I'm thinking of adding another. Remorse."

She cocked her head and he continued, "To remind me that I've already paid the price, and that it's time to put the shame and guilt behind me."

Once again her hard, tough-guy biker blew her away with his insight.

"That's beautiful." She kissed him, sealing her lips to his. Gentle but urgent.

———

COBRA KICKED open her bedroom door, then sat on the edge of the bed with her still in his lap. She wriggled to a standing position then leaned in and undid the button and zipper of his jeans.

He couldn't take his eyes off her as she slipped her hand past his briefs, cupping him, making all his pain disappear. His already hard dick got harder. As if that could even be possible. The power this woman had over every part of his body amazed him.

She fell to her knees in front of him and he pulled her up. "Nah, baby this night is all about pleasing you."

He hooked his fingers in the waist of her jeans, undid them, then pushed them down over her hips. He licked his lips at the sight of her curves front and center, all for him. He kissed her belly and she shuddered, and when he moved lower she arched her back. Inviting him, telling him what she wanted.

She reached up to him. "I want your mouth on me, and then I want you in me."

"Yes, ma'am."

He prowled up the bed nipping and sucking on the insides of her thighs. Leaving his mark, letting her know that she was his. She squirmed under him and he knew what she wanted, but maybe he'd make her wait a little longer to torture her.

"Baby, please," she pleaded.

"Gotta make you suffer a little after almost giving me a goddamn heart attack before." She narrowed her eyes and he smirked. "All right, you've suffered enough."

Truth. He wanted to taste her just as much as she wanted him there. Lapping his tongue against her, feeling her move with him. Best fuckin' thing—Ever.

He worked her and brought her to the edge, then stopped to gauge her body, knowing what she liked and how to make her feel every ounce of pleasure. Her fingers gripping his hair made his dick ridiculously harder. He gritted his teeth until his jaw ached, willing his body to hold on until the pain and pleasure became too much.

"Gotta get in you, babe," he ground out.

When she flipped over and pushed her ass in the air the little blood left in his brain shot right to his dick. "Fuck, yeah."

He gripped her ass with both hands, then bit each ass cheek. She yelped again and his dick twitched. She wiggled that beautiful ass and he moaned out. "Shit, baby, you're not playing fair." He fisted himself, then positioned his dick between her cheeks.

She looked at him over her shoulder. "Do you remember what you said to me that first night at the Gold Mine?"

"Right now I can't remember my own name." He thrust his hips and she ground into him.

"You said I had an ass made to be grabbed with both hands."

"And I was right." He squeezed her ass cheeks together making the friction hotter, almost unbearable.

He pushed further until he felt her heat. All wet and ready for him. Her grin turned into a teasing smirk, like she knew exactly what she was doing to him. She wiggled her ass again and he smacked it, then hit into her so deep his eyes crossed. She pushed her ass higher, and he wrapped his hands around her thighs, holding her to him, putting her in the perfect position.

He thrust into her over and over, her moans are louder and he knew she was close. She ground her hips, and when she clamped down on his dick he felt it. She pulsed and shattered around him, pushing him, begging him for all he had to give. He pounded into her harder and yelled out as his body exploded. The sensation of taking her raw exceeded anything he'd ever experienced with a woman. His woman.

The aftershocks and pulsing of her body continued for a few more seconds and he couldn't believe the sensations that flowed through him. All they'd been through in such a short time and she proved time and time again that she was there for him. Trusting him, caring for him, and he wanted to give her the same and more. Much more.

They collapsed together onto the rumpled sheets. He stroked her back and he swore he heard her purr.

She eased up on her elbow and traced the words tatted over his abs. "I think this is a very good time to finally tell me the meaning of this tat."

He sucked in a deep breath. He'd put her off because he wasn't sure he could put the new meaning into words.

"What's the matter?" she asked.

"The original reason, and what it means to me now are two different stories."

"So, start with the original one."

"It had to do with me being president of the Serpents. Python had already gone through a lot of shit with his old club and didn't want the responsibility of being in charge. I said I'd take on the president seat but he wasn't convinced and challenged my commitment to what we were trying to build. The result was this tat. Ride Till I Die."

"And now?"

"It hit me the other day how much it sounds like you." He propped some pillows behind him. "Patching me up after the shit at Valley View, wading through my panic attacks and holding me together. You're my side chick. No matter what you're always by my side." He squeezed her hand. "And even though you pissed me off putting yourself out there for Vinnie, it was fuckin' loyal. You are Ride Till I Die."

She bit her lower lip, then swiped at tear and then another. "That's beautiful." She sucked in a shaky breath. "I want to get one to match it."

He stared at her unable to form the words to tell her how much he loved her idea—Loved her? Shit, where did that come from? He experienced the same emotion when he thought she'd been shot. Love—a word so foreign to him, the very thought shocked him stupid. He'd take it slow. Ease into it with her.

"You're gonna make an amazing old lady." The words flew out of his mouth without his permission. What the hell happened to easing into it and taking it slow?

"Oh no, I don't want any labels. Labels get people in trouble."

She mashed her lips together, but he didn't push her. He could barely explain the spiral of emotions that coursed through him right now, either. He'd put it on hold—For now.

EPILOGUE

The night of Vinnie's shooting Cobra stayed at Sheena's apartment, then insisted she come to his place. No way he was letting her out of his sight after everything that happened.

Two days later, Cobra sat at his kitchen counter, coffee in one hand, phone in the other while Sheena still slept in his bed. Thanks to his connections at Metro, he read a police report telling him Vinnie's body was found at the mouth the drainage tunnel that emptied out behind Ecstasy. Officials labeled it a gangland shooting, which meant they'd do the basic investigating and nothing more. A bullet in the balls and another between the eyes. Accurate assessment. The shooters were probably on a plane heading east before the sun came up.

Cobra scrolled to the previous document and reread Danny's toxicology report. Thanks to those same connections downtown he received the autopsy report in a few days instead of a few weeks. Danny died of respiratory failure the result of fentanyl in his system. Because of Danny's condition, the hospital assumed it was administered for pain. Ironic, Danny didn't have physical pain, and he never did a street drug in his life, yet he'd basically OD'd.

Brookdale denied giving him the patch. And they were right. Brookdale's lawyer already sent him a fancy letter excusing them from any wrongdoing, which Cobra signed without hesitation. Brookdale wasn't responsible, and even though they'd accepted Vinnie's fake identifications and let him into see Danny, it didn't matter. Vinnie was in the ground where he belonged. Cobra sucked in a deep breath. And maybe Danny was finally in a place without pain where his goodness was honored.

Cobra pushed himself away from the counter, and busied himself making more coffee. It would be the only thing that got him through this day—that and Sheena.

THE MEMORIAL SERVICE for Danny was beautiful, if a bit eclectic. Sheena stood beside Cobra and all the Serpents, along with many of the other Nevada chapters. Large men all dressed in black wearing their cuts, faces somber, crowded around the gravesite.

Because Cobra kept his brother a secret to protect him, none of them actually knew Danny, but were here as a show of respect for Cobra. And that in itself was a testament to Cobra's position and reputation in the biker community.

Then to round out an already distinctive group, there were about twenty women huddled together also dressed in black. Although the somber colors didn't hide their exquisite figures. Sheena remembered a few from her visit to Ecstasy, but noted Patrice was not one of them.

In true biker fashion they met at the Gold Mine for a

private party. The Serpents were determined to give Danny a sendoff fitting for their president's brother.

Over the last few days, Cobra's quiet demeanor unnerved her. She caught him reading something on his phone this morning, and the expression on his face chilled her. The rage he'd experienced when he first heard of Danny's death disappeared, and was replaced with a lethargic apathy. He'd been attentive and caring, but detached, and she worried that he was heading for a deep decline.

Daisy slung her arm around Sheena. "How're you doing?"

"I'm worried about him." Sheena watched Cobra accepting condolences from his biker buddies. "He's been unusually quiet and eerily calm."

"Give him some space." Daisy nodded to Joker. "They can be complicated, but the end result is worth it."

Sheena hugged Daisy close. Her best friend knew first-hand the intricacies of biker life.

They'd only been there an hour when Cobra came up beside her. "Let's get outta here."

"Are you sure? All these people are here for you."

"An open bar and free booze. They'll be fine." He grabbed up her hand, said a few quick goodbyes, and dragged through the lot like the place was on fire. He silently handed her a helmet, then mounted his bike and waited for her to do the same.

They passed the exit for his penthouse, and when he eased onto I-15 she was confused until she realized they were taking the same route he'd taken to his cabin on Mount Charleston. She willed her body to relax and enjoy the ride. The wind in her face and the crystal blue sky above them eased the tension of the last few days.

She knew riding calmed him and she hoped by the time

they reached the cabin he'd open up to her and release some of the anguish bottled up inside. The last time he brought her here he wanted answers from her about her past and now she hoped to get answers from him.

He descended the winding driveway to the cabin, and entered the garage. They dismounted the bike, and silently ascended the steps from the garage to the main rooms of the house. When they entered the living room, she was again taken with the beauty of the pine trees that surrounded his property.

Cobra motioned to the couch. "Sit down." His voice seemed strained and Sheena's intuition ramped up her heart until she could feel it in her throat.

He paced in front of her a few times, and it did absolutely nothing to soothe her nerves. He finally stopped and peered at her. "The last few days have been crazy as fuck. I lost my brother." He paused and sucked in a deep breath. "Then I thought I almost lost you."

She'd hoped they'd gotten past her conning him, but maybe he couldn't forgive her. Maybe—Oh God, if he was breaking up with her, she wished he'd just get this done.

"I asked you something the other night in your apartment, and when you didn't give me the answer I wanted, I told you I'd wait."

Shit, and now he was going to tell her that he'd changed his mind. That they wouldn't work, that he was setting her free. Her heart beat faster and a trickle of sweat surrounded her neck.

"But I can't wait. I want you to be mine, always. I want you to be my old lady."

A deep horrifying silence surrounded them. His crystal blue eyes pierced through her waiting for an answer.

Her assumption was dead wrong. He wanted her to make

a commitment. Something she'd hoped would happen. She'd dreamed about a man who cared about her, a man whom she cared about, but now that the reality stood in front of her she freaked.

She certainly had no good example of a sound relationship from childhood to draw from, but perhaps she could turn the bad karma around. Maybe she could finally grab something good for herself in the form of a tough biker with the perfect Hollywood face and a body that—Shit, she had to concentrate.

"I want to be yours too," she whispered. "But—"

"How about if I say you're the woman I want on the back of my bike and by my side, who has my back every step of the way?"

"That sounds to me like the definition of an old lady."

"Exactly."

"I thought you'd never ask."

He scooped her up off the couch. "Always the smart ass, but you still haven't answered me."

"Yes, I'll be that." She wrapped her arms around his neck. "I'd be proud to be your old lady."

"Ride Till I Die?"

"Absolutely." She planted little butterfly kisses up his neck.

"And there's one other thing."

Oh no, what now?"

"I love you."

She blew out a huge sigh of relief and cuddled into him. "I love you too."

THE END

I Need Your Help With a HUGE Favor!

I would absolutely love if you would consider leaving a review on Amazon. I read every review and, every one is precious to me. Thank you in advance, and thanks again for reading.

CLICK HERE TO REVIEW

FREE PREQUEL: Joker's Story

This is just my way of saying thank you for purchasing Beyond Remorse/Cobra.

There was still so much that needed to be uncovered about Joker's past, that I felt compelled to write his backstory. Now, all you have to do is hit the link, and you can uncover Joker's very complicated past.

Joker's Story Link

ALSO BY BARBARA NOLAN

Joker and Daisy's Story

BEYOND REDEMPTION

Read an Excerpt: https://amzn.to/3jBsxZH

Joker has one thing on his mind while he endures the steamy heat of Miami Beach. Meet up with the cartel and make the one last deal for his outlaw biker club that will set him and his son free forever.

Sounds easy until a chance meeting with a sexy, mystery woman screws with his plan. Only thing is, his mystery woman hates all things biker, has a score to settle, and their chance meeting was deliberate.

Daisy knows the cruel underside of life, but now the con woman extraordinaire has transformed herself into one of Miami's premier players. When her elaborate plan to set herself free of the game goes awry, Joker comes to her rescue, and she sees that maybe this bad boy isn't so bad.

Their passion escalates as they design her biggest con yet. Pit her murderous boss against his vicious club president while trying to save his son, and deal with the tumultuous heat simmering between them.

Joker and Daisy's world twists and turns until neither one is sure who's in control as they teeter on the edge of what they need and what they want.

Join Joker and Daisy as they take down Digger in:

REDEEMED/THE ULTIMATE SCAM

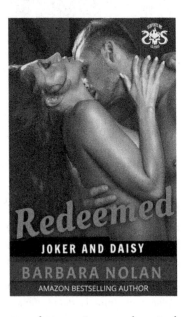

Joker tries to atone, but sometimes you have to do wrong for the right reasons in order to be REDEEMED.

The bait is dangled, and the lure is set for their biggest scam ever, so hold on tight as Joker and Daisy work together with the Serpents MC Las Vegas to take down a vicious enemy.

Find out what happens when you mix an outlaw biker set on revenge, a conwoman seeking redemption, and a ruthless psycho bent on retaliation.

If you love an angsty biker, and a sassy woman..

If you love the glitz of Las Vegas . . .

If you love a badass MC who's ride or die . . .

REDEEMED Is For You

Joker and Daisy's love is tested in:

Redemption/Joker and Daisy

Joker never believed in Redemption, he knew he was way past absolution, but having Daisy by his side evened out the bullshit.

Daisy could've given up on him in the bad old days, but she never did. She had a huge heart, smarts, and could easily pass for a runway model. What she saw in a scarred- up, ex-cage fighter, ex-drug dealer he never understood. They didn't even look like they belonged on the same planet, no less together, but her faith in him ignited a flicker of hope.

But hoping was a dangerous emotion, because it made you believe you deserved better. It sucked you in and swallowed you up. It made you forget that the good stuff could vanish in the snap of a finger. Suffocate in a poof of reality.

This is the continuing story of that hope . . .

Serpents MC Las Vegas

Beyond Redemption/Joker

Beyond Remorse/Cobra

Beyond Regret/Python

Redemption/Joker and Daisy

Redeemed

Beyond Retaliation/Boa~~ 6/21

Paradise Series

Beyond Paradise

Dangerous Paradise

Forbidden Paradise

Serpents MC Las Vegas Series

BEYOND REMORSE

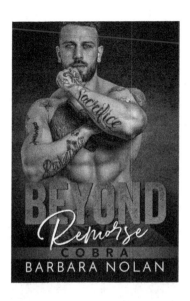

Read Excerpt: https://amzn.to/35JFxrg

Cobra and Sheena's Story

Cobra, the president of the Las Vegas Serpents MC, doesn't have time for distractions as he struggles to look after his handicapped brother, Danny, and keep him far away from the MC world. An old agreement with a greedy mob boss, helped pay for Danny's care, but dealing with the devil could put Cobra and The Serpents in jeopardy.

Sheena, the savvy, card hustler, is determined to go straight. Not so easy when the rent is due and your dinner is a bowl of cereal. Or when the same mobster holds secrets over your head, and refuses to set you free.

A biker wedding of mutual friends throws these two rebels together. Cobra knows peeling back Sheena's layers could be his biggest remorse, and Sheena knows the bad-boy biker with the crystal blue eyes could easily unravel her world, but a bottle of tequila later, he takes a very drunk Sheena home and tucks her into bed—Alone?

Fate thrusts them together, once again, when a heist goes wrong at an underground poker game Sheena is dealing. After an out-of-control night, of dodging bullets and eluding the cops, Cobra and Sheena fall into each other's arms neither caring about the consequences. Great if you believe in storybook endings, not so much if you're a realist who knows vicious fuckers never give up.

When the mob boss threatens Cobra's brother, and lures Sheena into his web, Cobra must take a stand. Protect his brother, or save Sheena from a life of crime.

BEYOND REGRET/Python

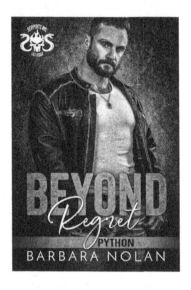

Read Excerpt: https://amzn.to/3fm7ysw

Python and Virginia's Story

Python has enough crazy in his life. Running Ecstasy, a high-end strip club for the Serpents, the random women that warm his bed, and the bookie breathing down his neck is more than the six-foot-five biker can handle. Until Virginia stumbles into his life.

A case of mistaken identity drops Virginia Swanson, a KLAS news reporter, into Python's apartment while he's celebrating his birthday, in his bedroom, with two other women. The flush in Virginia's cheeks, and the way the petite blonde stumbles out of his bedroom on her spike heels makes him smile.

These two opposites are thrown together again, and a night of sheet-gripping, lip biting passion ignites a thirst neither can quench, but the timing is all wrong.

Python's dealing with a whacko president of a rival MC, and a vindictive bookie who wants his fifty grand. So to keep Virginia safe, Python pushes her away.

Virginia has some secrets of her own, and when Python's life spirals out of control she may be the only one who can save him, even if it means giving him up.

Can Virginia come to Python's rescue in time, and prove to him that she's tougher than she appears? Or will Python conquer his demons both tangible and internal, and bring them both to a place Beyond Regret.

PARADISE SERIES/Mobbed Up In Manhattan

BEYOND PARADISE

Jonny Vallone, the dark, brooding owner of Manhattan nightclub, Beyond Paradise, doesn't need any more complications in his life. Then savvy con artist, Cheryl Benson, barges into his office and spits out a confession that would make most men run for cover.

Cheryl's fast-paced, out-of-control life is closing in, and bad boy, Jonny with his powerful connections might be her only hope against a ruthless crime boss. Her knight in black Brioni has a body made for sin with enough baggage to fill a 747, but when a near-fatal attack throws the two together, they implode in a night of steamy, sheet-gripping passion.

Their wild ride whisks them from the high-powered glitz of Manhattan to the sultry beaches of Miami in a desperate attempt to break free of their shady pasts while trying to tame their explosive passion and the dangerous deceptions swirling around them.

DANGEROUS PARADISE

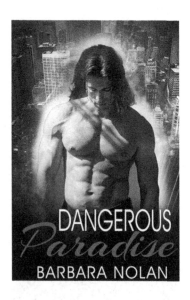

What do a Long Island heiress and a Harley-riding nightclub owner have in common? Absolutely nothing.

After an innocent dinner party goes straight to hell, Paige can't forget Eddie's gentle touch, or his deep rasp when he whispered in her ear. Eddie knows he's way out of his league with Paige, but damn he can't get her out of his head.

Can Paige take a walk on the wild side without getting hurt?

Can Eddie gamble everything he's worked for to keep Paige in his life?

FORBIDDEN PARADISE

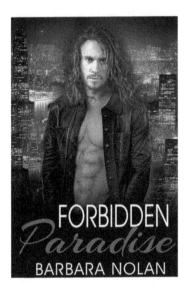

Dylan Benson, car thief extraordinaire, knows he has to make some solid changes in his life, but then Lena Vallone, and her desperate, ebony eyes turn his whole world sideways.

Lena is eager to escape the controlling ways of her wealthy older brother but taking his Maserati and going to a dive bar in Brooklyn isn't the best decision. Especially when she interrupts the theft of the custom car by an intriguing carjacker with haunting, silver eyes and an air of innocence—Like someone dropped him into this life of crime by mistake.

The two never expect to see each other again, but when her

powerful brother seeks retribution, she steps up in Dylan's defense and pleads his case. Dylan promises to reform, so to please Lena, her brother gives Dylan a job with one stipulation—Stay away from Lena.

Dylan is determined to turn his life around, but he can't ignore the simmering passion between him and Lena, or the threats from his thug friends unhappy with his new career choice. Maybe living the straight life isn't as easy as Dylan thought.

As pressure mounts, the chemistry between them sizzles. Keeping their relationship a secret is hard, but keeping Lena safe from his underworld ties might be deadly.

ABOUT THE AUTHOR

Barbara loves her emotional, passionate alpha males and the women who tame them. Her writing is sexy, spicy and seductive, and her goal is to have fun while taking the reader away from their world and into hers.

She is proud of this second act in her life and loves meeting and getting to know her readers, fans, and all the wonderful people in the writing community.

Her passion for reading and words make this a journey of love. She considers reading a luxury and writing a necessity.

KEEP IN TOUCH
Website: http://www.barbaranolanauthor.com

 twitter.com/bforlenza5
 instagram.com/bnolan26

Made in the USA
Columbia, SC
08 June 2021